95   96   97 98 99

ILL FEB '98 4
ILL JUL '98

Synonym for Love

Alison Moore

MERCURY HOUSE · SAN FRANCISCO

A portion of this novel was published in different form in *Ms.* under the title "Aperture." Another portion originally appeared as "Leaving by the Window" in the short-story collection, *Small Spaces between Emergencies,* Mercury House, 1992.

"Driftless" © 1994 by Greg Brown, from the CD "The Poet Game," reprinted with the permission of Red House Records, Inc., St. Paul, MN.

Published in the United States by Mercury House, San Francisco, California, a nonprofit publishing company devoted to the free exchange of ideas and guided by a dedication to literary values.

United States Constitution, First Amendment: Congress shall make no law respecting an establishment of religion, or prohibiting the free exercise thereof; or abridging the freedom of speech, or of the press; or the right of the people peaceably to assemble, and to petition the Government for a redress of grievances.

Mercury House and colophon are registered trademarks of
Mercury House, Incorporated

Designed by David Peattie
Printed on recycled, acid-free paper
Manufactured in the United States of America

— *Library of Congress Cataloging-in-Publication Data* —

Moore, Alison, 1951–
Synonym for love / by Alison Moore.
p.   cm.
ISBN 1-56279-074-9
I. TITLE.
PS3563.O568S96   1995
813'.54 — DC20   94-40442
                                              CIP

FIRST EDITION
5   4   3   2   I

ACKNOWLEDGMENTS

What began in solitude ended in collaboration. I am deeply indebted to my "eleventh-hour editor," Kore Salvato. For a short but intensely productive time, we became Wordsworth and Coleridge in Tucson, with daily conversation and the steady labor of bringing to the surface the organic whole, the underlying structure that needed only a steady hand to bring it to light.

I also want to gratefully acknowledge the National Endowment for the Arts, for a fellowship that helped to complete this novel.

There are others I would like to thank: Tom Christensen and everyone at Mercury House for unflagging faith; Janet Kaye for espresso and moral support; Chris Bondante and the dogs for necessary human and canine distraction; Mary and Aldo for the ranch in Tubac where much of the early revision took place; the alumni of Warren Wilson for annual reunions and Motown dances and late-night camaraderie; my sister, Sandra, who, though not embodied in a character, is nevertheless present between every line; Charlie Baxter — teacher, friend, listener; Tom Ives for all the journeys; the people of Lamalera, Indonesia, who taught me inadvertently about home; my students, from whom I continually learn; and finally, Stephen, for last-minute changes — not in the manuscript, but in my life.

For my mother, who left too soon;
  for my father, who stayed as long as he could.

Synonym for Love

Driftless

Have I done enough, Father,
can I rest now?
Have I learned enough, Mother,
can we talk now?
Will you visit me
in my place of peace?
I'm going driftless.

Let's cry all our tears,
cry them all out now.
Let them flow down
and clean all the rivers.
And the evening sky
is the reason why
I'm going driftless.

Have I worn enough clothes
to go naked?
Have I told enough lies
to see some truth?
Round hill — round thigh
round breast — round sky
I'm going driftless.

— Greg Brown
from "The Poet Game"

I drive through Death Valley at ninety miles an hour — a fugitive from an old idea of love. No one is chasing me. No one is even looking for me. All I know is that I want to get to the other side, wherever that is. There is no grass there, but if there were, it would be greener, I'm sure. The Ford pickup and I hit our stride together — there are things behind us now; we are heading *toward*. The wind is warm through the open window. My hair flies around me — the first thing about me that feels the freedom of the road.

By my calculations, I'm in the midst of the Chocolate Mountains. I look at these volcanic teeth and laugh at the whimsy in the name. The truck shudders. The "E" on the gas gauge really means what it says. An omen, a fitting, perfect little defeat, right on the California state line. I lean against the steering wheel as the truck rolls off the shoulder. I lean harder in surrender and the horn blares, as if the truck itself is shouting at me. My father would smile, sympathetically, I think, to see that I've gambled and lost. He taught me that game with the gas tank, and we've both bet against emptiness to see how far we could get on next to nothing. This is only the second time I've lost.

I get out of the truck, shield my eyes with my hand. The tinted windows held some of the glare back, but now the full force of the Mojave Desert hits me — the heat swarms above the highway and the sky will not take back what the sun has thrown down. I feel as if I'm swimming in fire, my body sluggish in air at least twenty degrees hotter than the blood that slows to syrup in my veins. Two signs face in opposite directions. I make my way between them and read: WELCOME TO CALIFORNIA, WELCOME TO NEVADA. The calcified dirt the posts are pounded into and the vista behind each — ragged, iron-gray mountains, blasted earth, sky a blue metal tempered flat and hard by heat — are exactly the same. "So this is where you've gotten to." I actually say this out loud because I think I need to hear it.

I take out my Polaroid. I place it carefully on the hood of the Ford and set the self-timer. I take a portrait of myself in between two indistinguishable states of America. There is approximately twenty feet between them, and I wonder who it belongs to. I claim it as my own. This is where I should be living — am living — between the lines. Exempt from taxes, laws, restrictions, speed limits. And history. Especially history. I can make up my own anthem and slogan, pick a state bird, a flower, a flag. I will be the entire population of the Land of Neither Here nor There.

The Polaroid spits out the photograph like a sticky black and white tongue; it dries instantly in the heat. The image hasn't finished darkening into a recognizable picture before a couple in a Winnebago heading west stops to give me their extra can of gas. I marvel at the people in the world who are prepared, who travel with maps and spares, who will not be set back very long by any emergency.

The house I have keys to now is hard to see, even when I'm almost in spitting distance. My new temporary home is single-story adobe, pinkish brown, camouflaged by the surrounding pinkish-brown hills, so different from the looming, three-story, bright blue, Queen Anne Victorian where I've been living in San Francisco.

I've answered an ad in a photo magazine to house-sit a place with a darkroom for the summer. I still can't believe I did it — picked up the phone and talked to a perfect stranger to get directions to a place to live. I'm tired of even my own address and now I have to start using someone else's. I've decided to believe in pilgrimage, trial by fire in the desert, visions. Probably just another cliché, but say what you want, it calls to me. To *me*.

I unload my truck of all my worldly belongings, absurdly few. I've been traveling light for so long it all fits into two suitcases and a duffel bag, not including an extra suitcase full of exposed film — my summer project. The rest of my belongings are supposed to be stored in a church basement in Virginia. God alone knows if they're still there.

I take a postcard from the dashboard. My brother, Jack, sent it recently from Guadalajara, Mexico, where he's been living for the past seven years. He wrote all was well — wife, kids, etc. — and at the end, almost as an afterthought, "Hard to stay put, isn't it?" He meant it, too, for both of us. I've been chasing my own tail for as long as I can remember.

Motion is not something I question; it's just what I know
how to do, how to keep doing.

I pace the house like a cat mapping new territory. I open
and close cupboards. The inside is eerily similar to places
I've tried to live in. Little in the way of comfort or decora-
tion — a couch, a bed, a table, a chair. No paintings or
posters, not even a calendar, just windows looking out to
the desert and the sharp mountains that burn lurid red in
the late afternoon light.

Carrie Silver, the woman who owns this place, is obviously a woman who doesn't cook much more than soup or
coffee for herself, and I imagine her as silver and mysterious as her name, an ascetic haunting her own bare house.
The darkroom, however, is well stocked, but there's no evidence of the work she does here — no photographs on the
walls, not even any rejects in the trash. Maybe she, too, can
no longer bear to look at her work anymore and needs to
travel to set her straight again.

I try to shake off the road, the roar still in my ears. I'm
cold. Frozen solid, through and through and through,
despite the eighty-degree midnight heat. I'm exhausted,
too. At times like this, when I'm too tired to move, people's
voices, memories, images catch up with me. I can see my
father, punching the horn for emphasis when he delivered
one of his highway "sermons." He loved to quote Robert
Louis Stevenson: "It is a better thing to travel hopefully
than to arrive." Now that phrase sounds as tired as I am.
Both Stevenson and my father are probably still doing it,
quoting high-minded phrases and traveling together in the
endless hereafter. All that hopeful travel has piled up, accu-

mulated deep within my body, and even as I try to fall asleep, every muscle, every ligament that strings me together knows: I've come to the end of the road, I'm losing the hope. I have arrived.

I sleep with all my clothes on; in a half-sitting, half-lying position on the sagging horsehair couch, counting white lines.

I attempt to establish a simple routine, to get up early, before the heat, but somehow I manage not to be able to drag myself out of bed until ten. I sit, slumped in a wicker chair on the patio, drinking strong, black coffee.

"You made your bed, Madame Butterfly, and now you will have to lie in it." My father again. I cover my ears. His words break through even the steady shrill whirring of hundreds of cicadas in the palo verde trees.

When I was a child, my father took me everywhere with him while he went on the road selling advertising for a travel magazine. He'd pontificate as he drove, in a voice pitched to Old Testament diatribe. He was not particularly religious, just deeply suspicious. There were signs everywhere, he said, and the gods grew angry if mortals ignored them. Hubris demanded retribution — this was the balance of the world, the one he staunchly believed in. "Love," he said, "will take you soaring, then bring you to your knees." The gods, it seemed, enjoyed the spectacle of romantic passion, let you have it for a little while before they took it back. My mother, by contrast, had remained silent, enigmatic, moving in and out of the searchlight of all his tightly focused desire. But she listened. If she had opinions on his philosophy, she never expressed them — at least to me. I watched from the sidelines, my lips sealed, my voice ricocheting off the empty, crowded place inside my heart.

I've given up trying to make a story of it. Once, in the seventh grade I actually tried to write some of it down, the part about my father not believing my mother died when she did, how he said the gods had taken her back again and that he wouldn't rest until he found her. The essay came back with a note in red pencil from the teacher saying I didn't follow the assignment, that I was plagiarizing Greek mythology, that what she wanted was an essay about something that really happened. I excused myself from the classroom and ran pell-mell down the hall to the only place I could go — the hollow, echoey sanctuary of the girls' room where I sat in a stall and fumed, until in final desperation, I wrote "Fuck you!" on the tiled wall. Then, as an afterthought, I signed my name. The words had a kind of graphic, indisputable power and they shouted continuously, shouted everybody down. Of course, I ended up with a scrub brush and cleanser the next morning, scouring the words and my name away. Still, they had their echo, have it still — have moved beyond the judgment of seventh grade and followed me around like a pushy cat that I'd made the mistake of feeding once and am bound to keep forever.

This desert patio becomes my perch. I can survey this desolate kingdom from a folding chair. I watch the neighbor, at least I assume it's the neighbor — the only one for miles — walk down the hill at ten to get her mail, one hand on the top of her wide-brimmed hat to keep the wind from snatching it away. With the other hand, she waves across a space too wide and wind-filled for conversation but narrow enough for signals of the hand. I wave back. She's old. Really old. For a moment I worry that she'll discover me, latch on to me, that she'll be some lonely old widow who will talk my ear off and I'll never get anything done. But in the determined way she walks by my driveway without even a casual glance at the house, she looks like someone who has no intention of coming any closer.

It doesn't take long to see that she has rituals. She takes that walk daily down the dirt drive that bisects her hundred and seventy-five acres of desert. She never drives. She has groceries brought in twice a week by a store that delivers.

I have been sitting on this porch every morning for two weeks now, waiting until Della Wolff (at least that's the name on the letters in her mailbox) makes her trip down the hill. Her wave is a benediction, and each day after I receive it I think I am ready to go into the darkroom and start working.

But I don't. I look at the contact sheets I brought with me, and I'm appalled at how many images there are of things I don't understand, fragments of meaningless objects. The more I look at them, the less sense they make, and I can't remember why, exactly, I took them, what in the world I thought I was seeing. A master's degree in photography from Berkeley has screwed up my vision, ruined my ability to compose objects in interesting ways inside a 35mm frame. Photography used to hypnotize me — what I saw through the lens was as charged and unforgettable as something witnessed through a keyhole. Now I feel as if I'm going blind, looking at the world with the urgency of

someone with a fatal affliction. Something is happening to
me — for some reason I think about dying alone in this
house, about the fact that no one would even know.

I will also lose my ability to speak if I don't try to have an
intelligent conversation, soon. I want to talk to someone. I
want to talk to Della. I walk to the mailbox and wait for her
to come down the road.

"Hello!" I call out. The wind pushes the word behind
me. I call out again, and she turns, holding her hat to her
head.

"Hello," I say once more, too loudly. She shouts at me,
"You don't have to yell!" She looks at me disapprovingly,
eyes narrow in suspicion, as if I'm trespassing, a stranger
here to sell her something, or take something away.

"Della," I say in a normal speaking voice. "I'm house-
sitting for Carrie Silver."

Her eyes travel to my feet and stay there. "How do you
know my name?" She glances at the house. "Houses take
care of themselves. You don't strike me as someone who
sits for very long."

I'm aware that I'm shifting from one foot to another, a
jumpy balancing act, an old habit. God knows what I'm
doing with my hands. I try to imagine what I look like: a
towering girl, her body blurred by baggy clothes, a mass of
unkempt hair, jet-black sunglasses with rhinestones on the
rims. I probably look like some has-been movie star to her,
someone desperate and washed-up and on the run.

She stands stock-still. Clear, ice-blue eyes, silver hair —
long and swept up beneath the hat. A few strands escape
the pins, float free on her slender, wrinkled neck. It occurs

to me she is beautiful. Ancient. Maybe even elegant. She holds herself in an offhand way, like a person long accustomed to her body yet mindful too of the way she carries it, a precious thing.

"It's Sunday," I say. "No mail today." Immediately, I regret it.

She eyes me warily, as if I've questioned her sanity. "Doesn't matter — I walk anyway."

The next thing just tumbles out of my mouth — I certainly haven't planned it. "Why don't you stop by for something to drink? I think I have some iced tea or something. Or I can make some."

"No, thank you," she says, then turns to go.

I can't believe she refused such a simple invitation.

"You can stop by this afternoon," she calls over her shoulder. "Four or five, whatever, I don't care."

She doesn't care. She doesn't wait for an answer, either. I stand there fidgeting, more unsure of her now, and watch until she disappears around a curve.

At four or five or whatever I make my way up the steep hill. Fifty feet from Della's house I find a half-finished stone arch, flanked by walls. The path leading up to it is made entirely of the round glass bottoms of bottles set into the ground like lenses that might afford a view into the center of the earth. At first it seems clever, even endearing, then a little crazy when it dead-ends at a free-standing wall, this half-finished arch, studded with a weird array of odds and ends: a handless face of a clock etched with Roman numeral hours, a toy pistol spewing silver bullets at a model of a

B-52. A gray-green television tube, blank as a glass eye. Blue
marbles and ball bearings. Bottle caps. The inner workings
of a pocket watch. Pot shards and spark plugs. Tiny flat
sieves of bathtub drains.

I move past the arch at a snail's pace, running my hand
across all of these things to feel their textures and surfaces
as well as see them. There's nothing, it seems, that she
won't stick into cement, and clearly, she doesn't give a
damn about trying to make sense. I stop at the end where
she's signed her work by pressing both hands, thumbs
touching, into the wet mud. "DELLA 1976" is written huge
above it, a little lopsided, almost a childish scrawl. I press
my right hand in the gray indentation. Her fingers are as
long as mine.

Behind the wall, an incompatible herd of clay animals —
a penguin, a heron, a javelina, a horse — all bending to
drink from a water-filled clay pot. Behind them, a kind of
concrete teepee at least ten feet high, constructed entirely
from mortared bottles — brown, blue, clear. I look inside,
bending through a "doorway" that looks hammered out,
the cement and bottles broken through. Light pours into
the vaulted space — pours through the down-tilted necks,
pooling a mosaic of color onto the cement floor around the
charred leavings of a fire. What does she do, sit in here,
summoning holy visions? I look up. Blue sky stares through
the smoke hole like the round eye of God. Then a raven
passes over, blinking the eye for less than a second before it
goes blue again.

Behind a tilting stone bench, an ironwood tree quivers
with bees. I sit there calmly enough, but my body shakes —

not with fear of being stung, but with an odd kinetic elec-tricity. I look around me, daunted by all this enterprise, wondering how it is that I am so empty-handed.

I just stay there a while, bees bumping against my hair. I hear music, I think, and running water from what must be the open kitchen window of her house. I believe she might be singing.

"Stop skulking around out there and come to the house," she calls. I'm not aware that I've made any sound at all. I see her through the branches, beckoning me toward the patio. My body rises, drifts toward her. She stands by a set of ice cream parlor chairs flanking a table, all of them painted aqua and Bengal rose. She holds a tall glass of something in her hands. Maybe it's because of the setting — that odd garden filled with manifestations from a strange mind, but suddenly I think of evil queens, ones with potions and ulterior motives, and I am afraid, both of approaching her and of letting her down by saying the wrong thing, whatever that might be. She holds out the glass of perspir-ing iced tea to me, not gracefully, with those sculptor's long fingers, but roughly, between clenched hands. And then I get a good look at her hands, at the havoc of knuckles and too-big bones, the hideous trespass of rheumatoid arthritis.

"I don't usually have visitors," she says. "I forget what I look like until people stare." She paused. "Like you. It's rude, you know."

I sit down with my tea in one of her chairs, embar-rassed, as if I've been caught cheating on a test or failed to bring my homework.

"Sorry," I say lamely, even a little defiantly, and now what I'm really sorry about is that I've come in the first place, that I've subjected myself to her cranky accusations. If she's trying to pick a fight with me, she's barking up the wrong tree. I don't like debates — I learned from my father a long time ago that I couldn't hold my own.

She hooks her index finger around a straw and pushes it into her glass. "Want one?" she asks.

I can agree to this, and it seems that the offer is an attempt at being generous, perhaps making up for her off-putting remarks. We sip our tea slowly. The amber liquid races up the clear plastic, slides back down again.

I look around for the first time at the fieldstone house, at the several chimneys, each a different shape.

"I built this place myself. Still building it. Did you see that arch when you came in? When I get that done I'm making an arbor."

I can't imagine making something on such a large scale, something as tangible and permanent as a wall. "How in the world did you do all this?" I ask.

"One stone, then another one." She sucks noisily at her tea. "You probably don't approve. What's the word you people have nowadays — kitsch." She sucks the glass dry. "Who cares? I'm not trying to get a Guggenheim. There's just myself to please." She sets the glass down on the table, and it nearly tips over. She swipes at it with her gnarled hand to steady it, and it teeters precariously before it somehow manages to right itself. "What about you — what are you doing down there on your own? Who are you trying to please?"

"I don't have anybody to please." The last question is easier to answer than the first. What *am* I doing down there? I don't feel like going into it — there's too much to tell, or not enough, so I give her the short version, which is just the facts. "I came here to work in the darkroom, but I think I've forgotten how. I'm not getting much done. I don't know what's the matter with me." But as I say these things they sound so bald I wish I'd kept my mouth shut. Still, it silences her, at least for the moment.

Della looks as if she wishes she hadn't asked, and changes the subject. "Any family around here?"

"Not anymore. My brother's in Mexico. My parents are no longer living." Just saying this makes me feel orphanish, small, bereft, and I wonder what it is in me that makes me suddenly both long for and dread her sympathy.

"Family gets in the way. I got rid of mine." She shifts in her chair, crosses one of her long legs over the other. Her calves are tightly muscled, the skin translucent over dark blue veins.

"I suppose that's interesting work, photography," she continues, "if you like that sort of thing." She's baiting me. I'm not biting. But she doesn't wait for me to counter; she's back to her inimitable self again. "I couldn't stand being cooped up in the dark all the time. Everything I do is out-of-doors in broad daylight."

I stir the ice around and around in the glass with my straw. I pretend to be intent on this mindless task. My leg jitters in time to some restless percussion inside me. Della stares at it as if by scrutiny alone she can make it stop. She only makes it worse.

I think of this woman moving purposefully, even defiantly, from one thing to another, in no particular hurry. Getting useful advice from her is probably a long shot, but I have to ask her, even though I don't think she'll give me the answer. "Are you ever afraid — you know — that you'll wake up one day and find you've run out of ideas? Like maybe you used them all up? Or had them to begin with, but blew it somehow? Do you know what I'm talking about?"

"Nope," she said, taking a last noisy pull on her tea. "Is that happening to you?"

"I hope not — I don't know — I think it probably is."

"You shouldn't be worrying about that already — that's for people my age to lose sleep about, people who are running out of time. What are you, twenty?"

"Nearly thirty."

"No wonder."

A coyote starts up, just below the hill. Another soon joins it. I'm grateful for the interruption. I don't want to know how she's confirmed her opinions about me.

"The Greek chorus," she tells me. "Except they don't give advice, which is just as well, even though they're smart. According to the legends, they're notorious liars."

We listen for a while. It's hard to tell how many there are — more than ten, or only two. They stop as suddenly as they started.

"When I was twenty-six," Della says, "I left my husband sitting in Chicago with a very surprised look on his face. It's a time in your life to start throwing things over the side, like sand out of a balloon." She thrusts her arm out as if she's literally throwing something over the side. Her hand, however, is immobile at the end of it, the fingers grafted to her palm. "It's hard just to rise," she says, moving her arm gracefully, oblivious of her misshapen hand.

We watch the sun go. It's the last distraction. It drops below the mountains fast, but the light it leaves behind takes a long time to change places with the dark.

"When my husband was alive — that's over twenty years ago — he'd come out here to visit since we'd lived separately most of our married lives. He preferred Chicago, worked there selling life insurance, of all things — as if you could buy yourself more time! He'd come out here and ask to see what I'd made, not so much because he liked my work, but I think he wanted to see some evidence of production. I don't think he ever understood what I did with all my time. I don't think he ever appreciated the idea that you could sit here and look out over these hills for an entire afternoon, that just noticing what the birds did could be more than enough for one day."

Della sighs, shifts forward in her chair. My audience with her, it seems, is over.

"So what did you do?" I ask, trying to keep her just a little longer.

"Do?" She stands up, stiffly, unbending herself by degrees. "I sent him home." She looks behind her at the house, as if it's calling her back in, as if she's spent long enough outside of it with a stranger.

"It's like rain," she says, turning back to me again.

"What is?"

"What comes and goes — like water in these empty riverbeds after a storm. You can only catch a little of it, but it soaks in. And it doesn't happen unless I'm alone."

"Oh," I say, twisting in the chair. My leg is still bouncing. "You mean ideas comes to you like rain — not a great analogy in this part of the world. This — desert." I point at the whole arid spectacle of it that is only briefly stanched by these chairs, this patio, this house.

Della bursts out laughing. "You wait. You just wait."

I can't wait. I don't have the patience for this cryptic game. The next words fly out of me so fast it sounds as if I'm chiding her, which I feel I've earned after all I've endured. "You sent your husband home because he didn't understand you?"

"He tried. It's too much to ask of love that another person understand you. It's hard enough to just be tolerant."

I don't have a comeback, not to these riddles. I don't know enough about love to know what can be tolerated or understood because of it. Or what is precious about solitude — some part of me still feels that someone or something must always be forsaken because of it. The word forsaken scares me, its bigness, its boundless implications. I have to push hard against it to get it out of my mind.

"I'm not saying you have to be alone — it's what turned out to be true in my life." She turns toward the house. "Did you bring a flashlight?" she asks.

"Do I need one?"

"Not unless you don't want to step on a snake. I've got an extra — I'll lend it to you."

When she comes back out of the house, a cone of light precedes her on the ground. She passes it to me.

"Watch yourself," she says as I turn to go.

I see only one snake, or what looks like the shape of one, disappearing into the brush, moving as if pulled slowly forward on a string by a patient, curious hand.

I dream that night that I lure my mother out of heaven with a personals ad. The ad reads, "Auralee, please come back, all is forsaken." Even in the dream I know that the right word is "forgiven," that I have mixed in the day's words with the night, that the word I pushed down earlier found its way to the surface again. In the dream I wait for my mother in a Greyhound bus station. I lie down naked on a wooden bench. Buses come and go. Finally she arrives, but she walks right past me without looking once in my direction. I have no words to call myself to her attention.

That dream follows me around for days. I try to erase the images in my head with real ones that come through the lens. I walk around in the desert shooting endless rolls of film. Cactus, clouds, rocks — it doesn't matter as long as it's tangible. I work frantically, long into the night, to print the images, as if they might dissolve like ancient artifacts in the caustic, modern air. I stumble back into the world at 2 A.M., exhausted, my fingers stinking of chemicals, my cuticles raw.

After one of these marathon darkroom nights I walk barefoot onto the patio. A lemon-wedge moon hangs low over Della's house, shining in her windows, which are dark. The air is absolutely still.

When a sharp pain stabs my foot, I know without looking that I've stepped on a scorpion. I watch in horror as it skitters away. Should I get myself to the emergency room

— should I call an ambulance — will I slip into a coma from some freak reaction to the poison the way some people swell and die of a simple yellow-jacket sting? Della, I am sure, will know what to do.

I take the truck, get myself up the hill driving as fast as I dare, lurching over washboard and potholes, and somehow have the presence of mind to swerve to avoid a jackrabbit racing across the road. Once at the house, I stumble for the door, even more terrified now that the hot, stinging pain crawls faster up my leg. I imagine a red poison coursing through my veins aiming straight for my heart.

I pound on the door with both fists. "It's me, Matty." I pound again, louder. "It's Matty," I scream.

It takes her forever to get there. No locks turn. She simply opens the door and stands there holding a flashlight — a white, flowing shape in a nightshirt, her waist-length hair undone.

"What in the world is the matter with you?"

"I stepped on a scorpion."

"Is *that* all."

Too shocked to feel embarrassed, I yell, "Well it *hurts!*"

She brings the flashlight closer to my face and scrutinizes me, trying to decide whether I am telling the truth. She steps back. "I'm sure it does — I'm sorry. Here, never mind. Come in."

I limp behind her into the kitchen. She opens a bottle of vinegar with some difficulty. "Lift your leg up and put it there," she points, "in the sink." She pours the vinegar on the red welt. "There," she says, as if she's done all she can do.

I don't feel any particular relief, or even slightly taken care of. I stand there on one leg, the other in the sink, feeling utterly ridiculous, like some preposterous, awkward wading bird. The whole thing strikes me as so hard-boiled Western, like biting a bullet while your leg is cut off, and then watching someone cauterize the stump with a burning torch.

"Do you feel feverish at all?" She peers into my face but doesn't place her hand on my forehead.

"No," I answer, uncertainly. "Should I?"

"Probably not. You don't look like the type."

"What do I look like?" I wonder out loud, as if she alone in the world can see me clearly.

"You look like someone who could use a shot of whiskey." She opens a cupboard and pulls down a bottle of Jameson's. She starts to open it. "Here," she says, handing it to me. "You do it."

I take my foot out of the sink. Gingerly, I ease my weight onto it. I open the bottle and pour into the two glasses she's set on the counter.

"I have it for special occasions," she says. "This is special enough."

We knock the thick, blue Mexican glasses together, then sip the whiskey. It's sharp and hot, like the poison in my foot, but it goes down easy.

"I've been lucky that way — I've never gotten bitten by anything much except kissing bugs." She takes another swallow. "Kissing!" She sniffs.

She leads the way to the living room and doesn't bother to turn on the lights. We sit in two overstuffed chairs facing the window. The moon is almost gone.

"I got kissed more by bugs than I ever did by a man." Her voice comes out of the half-dark to me. I can't quite see her face, just the silver hair like a veil catching the light. There is no bitterness in her voice — it's just a thing she tells about herself, like an eccentric habit she's gotten used to. I want to tell her she isn't missing much, but I don't believe it. I just ended a two-year relationship that began with a lot of heat but ended at a frozen impasse. The kisses are still hard to get out of my mind.

"I remember it perfectly, though," she says, as if reading my thoughts. "Like singing without making any sound."

I whisper, "Yes. It's like that." I feel a little drunk with exhaustion and poison and whiskey. My foot still throbs, but it doesn't seem to be getting any worse. I lean my head back in the chair. I try to remember how it feels to be kissed, to kiss someone back you can't bear losing. A kiss. I fall past it, below it, to a time before a man's mouth came that close to mine, to a time when I could only wonder what it felt like, what it meant, why it looked like a hunger I didn't understand.

I imagine I hear Della asking me what they ask you in emergency rooms after trauma: Do you remember your name? Do you know where you are?

And I hear my voice coming from a long way away, though I don't remember moving my mouth, just these pictures, saying things, saying what they will inside me, whether I listen or not.

There was a summer, a summer my father and mother and I spent on the Shenandoah, when things were still whole, when no one was sick or grieving or leaving home for good. My father had rented a cabin from a man in Front Royal so near the river we could hear the slow surge of it in our sleep. My father slept on the porch because it was cooler, but my mother preferred to sleep inside away from the mosquitoes. I had the rollaway bed in the living room.

I felt her brush past, saw her white slip dimmed down to a gray shape that flowed through the room. The screen door hinges twisted slowly on their rusty springs. The night air strained through the screens. He was not asleep either. He lay waiting for her, hands beneath his head, elbows framing his face like half-folded wings. She stood in the doorway, one ear tuned to me. I feigned sleep, devised an exaggerated rhythm of breathing. It satisfied her. My eyes wide open, I watched her turn to the anticipated music of my father, a song she half knew by heart, still compelled by the notes she didn't know. Even in the dark she could find him. Her fingers could trace the well-known path, the jawline from ear to chin, and she would be able to predict the slight bump on the bridge of his nose just before her fingers arrived. But if she continued, if her curiosity was piqued by the half-naked feel of her body outside the house, of my father waiting on the porch, she would explore until she found the variation she could not expect — some jut of bone, some hidden mole that would stop her fingers in their tracks, as if she were exploring his almost identical brother. I imagine it was the scar that did it, the surgeon's sloppy signature on his thigh — the thigh he'd torn open as a boy leaping across a spiked, wrought-iron fence. She always said she wished she'd been there to catch him.

Touching any scar is opening it. It's more like a zipper than a sealed ridge of skin. She would lean down, I think, her fingers only capable of reading a limited Braille, and let her lips intuit the rest. I watched her head lower, her hair swing like a curtain around the two of them.

I must have made a sound. Her head lifted, she turned her face back toward the house. She rose and the cot's springs lamented her departure. My father didn't make a sound. She came back inside, stood by my bed.

"Matty," she whispered.

I didn't know whether to answer, what it would mean if I did.

"What," I said sleepily.

Her hand, warm on my forehead, as if feeling for a fever. No, not her hand. This hand ran fingers through my hair.

"You were dreaming," her voice said, but I felt the voice was no longer coming from her.

"Were you dreaming?" Della asks.

I try to hold on to the thought of my mother's hands, in the moonlight that summer on the Shenandoah coming down to touch me in places only she was privileged to know. But try as I might, the images, those hands, dissolve.

I dive down after my mother, her hands a lure, myself a fish willing to be caught. I call out. There's a hand on my forehead, a blanket around me. The moon is gone and Della's hair is no longer silver, but gray. She is going now, and I want to say don't go, don't you want to hear a story — not a fairy tale, not a made-up thing.

Like Scheherazade, I want someone to hear my story,

but no one threatens my life. It's my own body that's become an hourglass, everything sifting down, the words rise up in counterweight. Just let me begin.

My father's stories were always told to me in cars: first the Packard, then the Plymouth, then the Studebaker Hawk. The cars, like the stories, started out large, extravagant with detail, then narrowed over the years until they were small in scale and scope. We would go for long rides up and down Virginia, sometimes hundreds of miles, beginning in the year my mother took sick. The motion of the car seemed to hurry his thoughts, and he said things at that speed when the country was just a blur beyond the window, things he could never say in the stillness of the house.

"She's taken a turn for the worse," my father said one day as we drove the slow, curving spine of the Blue Ridge Parkway. She had been in a hospital bed for a month; I pictured the turn for the worse: my mother behind the steering wheel of our sky-blue Packard, left hand reaching out in the rushing air, signaling a turn. She leaves the smooth macadam for a steep, rutted road, and the car, so grand at high speed on a highway, bumps hideously, lurching through the ditch, coming to a halt in a stubble field.

That's the way I saw it, her turn for the worse, and for the longest time, and sometimes even now, I believed that if I could find that road where she turned off she would be there still — the Packard at a smooth idle — leaning back in the seat, smoking a menthol cigarette, the radio on, the Blue Ridge changing color through the windshield in the late afternoon until it lived up to its given name. I would get in and sit beside her; she would say she had never meant to get so far away.

I never got to visit her. In 1963 hospitals didn't allow anyone under eighteen in the cancer wards — they didn't yet know the disease wasn't contagious — and I was two years away from satisfying their rules. I ran away from home then. But her cancer was a bigger story than what happened to me, and what my father called "the grand adventure of the prodigal daughter" was forgotten. Her illness even upstaged Kennedy's assassination, at least in our house. While the country grieved, cancer claimed all of our attention; we prepared for the next onslaught of poison and radiation.

Six months to the day after she'd gone into the hospital, the school principal himself came to get me out of class and I knew right away what it meant. He didn't say anything, just took me to the glass doors in front of the school and said, "Your father's here."

His white Studebaker seemed so small squeezed in between two yellow buses. He leaned over and pushed the door open. I didn't want to get in, would rather have turned around and gone back to my eighth-grade homeroom and listened to Mrs. Baines talk about the Maya, how they made some sense out of the stars and came up with a calendar they could count on, how they had created a kind of safety and order in their lives when everything around them grew wild.

The radio was turned up loud and Patsy Cline was singing. My father practically had to shout over her. "We're going to the YMCA."

I turned the radio down. "But there's no water in the pool this time of year," I reminded him.

I wanted him to say something that made perfect sense, to make the day go back to being a regular Wednesday again instead of the kind of day when the world came undone, but he said, "Well, we're going to see about joining up in the spring."

There was a loose piece of vinyl stripping on the side of my seat. I pulled on it so hard that it opened a seam in the upholstery, and I buried my fingers in the soft stuffing.

He pulled into the parking lot by the swimming pool and didn't make a move to get out of the car. We sat there looking at the chain-link fence and just beyond it to the gaping blue-green cavity with faded black numbers counting off the depths — 3, 4, 8. The lifeguard's chair had a frayed cushion on the seat, and the ladder had somehow been removed so that the chair looked stranded between an empty pool and the wide-open sky. A loose blue-and-white awning flapped listlessly in the wind.

"Are you brave?" he asked.

I had to answer "Yes." No other answer seemed possible.

"Are you strong?"

I thought about a movie I'd seen, a blindfolded man standing in front of a wall and another man giving the orders to the firing line. The last cigarette took a long, long time. "Ready," and the pause. "Aim . . ."

My jaw clenched and I bit the side of my mouth, hard. My fingers groped in the stuffing until I found something metal to hold onto. I closed my eyes.

"Matty . . ." I felt him turn toward me. "Your mother

died last night." I couldn't look him in the face. "Are you listening? Please, Matty, don't make me say it again."

The night before she was buried my father and I broke into the funeral home. Maybe trespassed is a better word, for nothing was actually broken. The back window was unlocked and we simply climbed through it. It seemed as if we'd come to rescue her, but there were no guards, no alarms, just my father and me with pocket flashlights sneaking down the corridor of the Joyner Funeral Home. We could have been spirits ourselves coming to claim her, escort her out of the weight of the body, the earth, the very atmosphere that once sustained her. But we were breathing like living things, our bodies working perfectly with the blind accuracy of clocks.

I followed his dark shape into the room where she slept inside a brass-handled box, the lid propped open like the hood of a car. I let him go ahead to do whatever he came to do. It was as if some invisible barrier held me back — I could not go up to the casket to look at her. I was sure she'd have an expression that would be so final it would erase any other image of her I'd ever had. He said something I couldn't hear. He carried on a whole conversation with her in the dark and then bent down into the box and kissed her. I stayed by the doorway, my light extinguished, a willing handmaiden abetting someone in a secret encounter. The light from a streetlamp squeezed through the fat venetian blinds; the shadows of flowers arranged themselves into a tropical arboretum, their cloudy scent mingling toward a common perfume. She was allergic to perfume. I half expected her to sneeze in the red rose dark.

I sat down on a metal folding chair against the wall in the dark room, a single spectator in a mysterious pageant, watching the shadow of my father barely moving against the lighted screen of the blinds. This scene would play again and again in my life: my father acting like a man I no longer knew; me trying to interpret his character from a distance. I longed for the soft blur, the freedom of a similar amnesia, but I held fast to the sharpness of grief. My father, in that room, began to lose his shape. He traded in his solid structure for a wisp of wild thought. I saw it happen, as if she'd swayed him, whispered that the body could be exchanged for what it really wanted: to no longer be a body but a dream of the body, to enter into an everlasting state of languid repose.

I could not compete with her, would not compete with her, for that kind of attention, which I understood to be the single-mindedness of love, which I now know is the most contagious thing of all. With a fierce logic that both calmed and scared me, I gave him to her. "Here," I said, in silent assent. As if he were mine to bestow, as if she could still receive him.

We left, a solemn procession of two, back through the window that gave onto the dirt alley. But she followed us — I could feel it. She made her own escape before she could be buried in the ground. That night she left a trail so tangible I knew she could pull him anywhere.

The friction of gravel was reassuring. The grit of the

ordinary world beneath my sneakers instead of the deep plush of the parlor helped erase that feel, that floating world of the dead, barely contained within the flimsy walls of the funeral home. We got in the car, and he released the brake, let it roll forward without the thrum of pistons, and drove down the alley with the lights off, the Studebaker Hawk drifting until we nosed into the main street. He turned the key finally, and the engine woke up. He turned the headlights on, put the car in gear — rituals of preparation to enter the stream of the highway. But we just sat there at the stop sign. Finally he turned to me. "Would you mind driving?" I looked at him in alarm. "I don't think I can," he said.

I'd barely done more than drive the back roads when my father let me take the wheel, and was still a year away from getting my learner's permit, but that night I drove into the next county and the one after that. As long as I kept driving the night would last, the day of the funeral would be postponed. We listened to a station that reached us all the way from Memphis. A steady stream of Delta blues came down the airwaves, came directly to us through the single dashboard speaker. I imagined we were the only people in the world listening.

"It's Fate — that's what this is . . ." my father said, then paused for half a song, letting his thoughts trickle down the line to where he could speak.

I made myself wait for the rest and watched the black trees streaking by. Not a single light, not a soul anywhere in the world awake but us.

"She decided she had enough of a family, with you. She

wanted to stop. Who was I to say any different?" He sunk
down into the seat, rested his head against the back of it.
His voice was so small I had to lean toward him to catch
what he was saying.

"I drove her to Baltimore one night. I'd heard of a doctor there — at least he was supposed to be a doctor — but
there was no sign on the door." He stopped. For a minute
all I could hear was his breathing, slow but uneven. "I waited in this little room. I heard her cry out — the walls were
that thin. It took a while for the rest to happen — the cancer. Nine months. Like a false . . . pregnancy." That word
was the hardest for him to say. "A tumor, the size of a wal-
nut — that's the way the doctor described it. Think of it!" he
said. I tried not to. He leaned forward, bracing himself
against the dashboard as if he couldn't shake the image
from his mind. I looked at him sharply, afraid, and his face
contorted as he saw my face, and then he leaned back
against the seat again. I didn't want him to say any more —
I knew what was coming — but he was unstoppable.

"If she'd had it done by a real doctor in an actual hospital. If she'd never done it in the first place . . ." He stopped
talking. The car crept forward around a wide turn. Just
steering was holding me together but I couldn't do it
smoothly. I went around that curve as if black ice teased the
wheels. I could hear the succession of his thoughts coming
— Chinese boxes — each idea sheltering a more intricate
one. If she hadn't had an abortion. If she hadn't gotten pregnant. If he'd never touched her. If he'd never even met her,
she'd be alive this minute.

"Be careful," he said. At first I thought he was talking

about my driving and was relieved he was still with me, paying attention, that he could take the wheel if I needed him to. But he went on: ". . . of getting what you want. It gets taken away from you. You can't consort with the gods for long — they always strike you down, sooner or later."

The gods. Who were they and what did they want with us? He was always summoning them when he ran out of logic. I always thought being a journalist must have frightened him in some way — all that bad news to deliver to the world. I think that's why he studied mythology obsessively and had two shelves of books on the subject. In those stories he found faces, names for Fate. Who on earth could be blamed for anything when there were all those capricious deities who were hard to please, easily riled, vengeful as children? In my father's story, the one he made of his own life, he had offended them. And now there would be hell to pay.

I wished that he would stop thinking, stop going crazy. Stop making me listen to him. I dared a response. "None of this is your fault. None of this has that much to do with you."

"Oh, but it does," he said, strangely calm. "You have no idea." And then I knew he would stay with her. Always. Through his imagined complicity, through his hard faith in holding on to her particular kind of love, which neither in death nor in life was earthly or ordinary, but rather miraculous and doomed, orchestrated by the Fates who made them meet in the first place and then, tiring of the game, snatched her away.

At 4 A.M. I pulled, finally, into the driveway. We didn't

turn any lights on as we walked into the house. I felt for
him in the dark hallway. Every bit his height, I hugged him
and he let himself be held. I wished I were small enough to
be picked up, just this once, but everything was changing
quickly. Already I felt him sag beneath the weight of even
my slightest want. A want no bigger than a fleck that started to grow without my consent, that would not stop until it
had all of me.

My mother's funeral was presided over by Reverend
Payne, though he hardly knew her and probably had to
work hard to come up with some parting words that even
generally applied to her. Mrs. Timberlake, who'd played
the organ in the church for seventy of her eighty-two years,
reluctantly played the hymn my father had insisted upon —
"Shall We Gather at the River" — because it was the one
my mother had once sung to him when they swam in the
Shenandoah.

I'd driven with my father the two blocks to the church.
We could easily have walked, but the car gave us shelter, if
not a literal armor. At the last minute, I wouldn't leave it. I
sat there during the entire service and heard the music
from the open door of the church. "Shall we gather at the
river, the beautiful river of love." I imagined that the song,
to her, had nothing to do with God and everything to do
with desire. She never went to church, so I knew she sang it
as a joke. Just thinking of it made me smile. I leaned back in
the seat and propped my feet in their improbable black
pumps against the dashboard, watched a run crawl slowly
up my leg. For some reason, I was ravenously hungry and

devoured nearly a whole box of crackers my father had
wedged between the bucket seats. I had both windows
rolled down, and a small, blue butterfly flew in one window, then out the other.

Everyone came out of the church following the casket
as if it were a dark boat drifting downstream toward the
cemetery. The uneven height of the pallbearers made the
motion choppy, uneven. I ducked down so they wouldn't
see me — a reflex action that really made no sense since
they'd seen me sitting there on their way in. On the floor of
the car, inches from my nose, several bottle caps were
pressed flat like little silver seals into the mat. Some toll
stubs — one from the New Jersey Turnpike, another from
the Blue Ridge Parkway. Paper clips. Cracker crumbs. And
stuck beneath the passenger seat, my mother's favorite sunglasses, which she'd thought she'd lost and had lamented
loudly about for weeks — she called them her movie star
glasses. The frames were studded with tiny rhinestones. I
put them on, and the world dropped down into blue,
almost lavender, from the lenses. I inched my way up into
the seat again and sat facing the empty door of the church.
I adjusted the rearview mirror so I could see the procession
turning in at the cemetery gate. Through the tinted glasses
and the mirror, the scene looked eerie, surreal, like a dream
sequence in a movie. I could see my father, in a hat of all
things, not right behind the casket, but lagging at the rear.
He looked over his shoulder back toward the car. He knew
I was in it. And I knew he'd rather be in there with me than
where he was.

The graveside service didn't take long. Reverend Payne's

words, I'm sure, were hurried. Mrs. Timberlake swayed slightly beneath a black umbrella to keep the impending rain off and looked like a precarious black flower, thin-stalked, and top-heavy. If there had been a breeze, she sure-ly would have gone over.

My father was the first one to come out of the gate. I could see him in the mirror, standing there by the road. He took his hat off, set it on the gatepost. He looked more than alone. He looked cast out. The rest of the small group stayed to watch the casket lowered into the ground.

I slid into the driver's seat. He'd left the keys in the igni-tion. I started the car, gunned it, and the Studebaker Hawk lurched into reverse, actually spun gravel getting out of the church parking lot. I drove as fast as I dared to get to him. I could see the people making their way down the path toward him, and I raced to get there first. I screeched to a halt just past him — I'd miscalculated the stopping distance. The car shuddered and nearly stalled. I revved it hard, threw the door open.

He stood there, staring at the car. "Get in!" I cried. And he did. He snapped out of his trance long enough to scram-ble into the passenger seat. The car moved forward before he got the door closed. Reverend Payne's face was the one I caught a glimpse of — surprise turning so fast into concern. We left them at the gate, literally in a billowing cloud of red Virginia dust, which my mother's glasses turned a deep vio-let. My father looked wildly at me, and then I knew. He was staring at the glasses, at what he thought was my mother wearing them. My mother — come to rescue him from her own funeral. I couldn't help it. I began to laugh — a crazy, high-pitched laugh that veered dangerously toward hysteria and stopped just short of tears. I drove fast and hard in the Studebaker Hawk, almost believing we might leave the ground.

Three miles from town, just east of the highway that could have taken us anywhere, the Hawk sputtered and died. We'd run out of gas — something we never did because my father was so good at the game, at gambling against the gauge. He never lost. "I'm sorry," he said, and I knew how much he meant it.

That day he lost. And our big getaway, which I suppose you could say was doomed from the start, ended with us limping back to town. I carried my shoes in my hand the whole way home, but I hardly felt the blacktop on my stockinged feet. He stopped once to hang his coat across a fence. He undid his tie and let it fall across the rail. I wondered if he were leaving a trail, in case she needed to find him.

"Where were we going?" he asked.

"I don't know."

He nodded. "There's no telling . . . ," he said.

"It didn't seem to matter," I interrupted.

He finished, ". . . with a full tank, there's no telling how far we could have gone."

In the days that followed, I walked through the house, and everything my mother had ever touched held her fingerprints as if dusted by detectives with a mist of talc. The whorls and lines, like no one else's in the world, were everywhere, the unmistakable graffiti of her touch we didn't dare wash off.

He hardly came out of his room except to eat in silence what I put in front of him. He was there, but just barely. I knew it was only a matter of time before he would go. I believe I must have read several books, my time measured only by the slow turning of pages, though I don't remember their titles or a single image of the characters that populated their manor houses and towns.

It seemed to me then that my mother, too, had always been driving, always away. Our life as a family had never had a particular cadence; its rhythm, as soon as I'd picked it up, was always counterpointed by some wild riff. We'd moved at least once a year until I was twelve, had come to Virginia after Michigan, New York, Maine. Gypsies, people called us. Moving was something we were good at. At the time, I think I enjoyed all that change — there was no time to be bored. My mother had her own wanderlust, separate from my father's, and she left the first time when I was eleven. She drove when she became too restless to sit still. She always went to the same place, to Virginia Beach, and she'd always come back after a day or two. She once told me she'd always wanted to be a marine biologist, to know the names of everything that lived beneath the waves, but had ended up only being able to walk alongside them, bringing home shells she saved inside an old hatbox on the closet shelf.

She took books on marine biology out of the library and catalogued her findings as best she could. In her thirty-

eighth year, a biological process she understood only too
well began inside her, traveling, metastasizing to places
conducive to rapid growth: the liver, the brain itself, which,
despite its intimate knowledge of the lives of cells, was pow
erless to prevent its own invasion.

Three days after the funeral I was sitting on the porch
waiting for the mail when a red pickup with Arizona plates
pulled up in front of the house. A man got out. He was tall,
practically had to unfold himself to get out of the truck. His
hair was jet black and half his face was masked behind a
beard. His jeans had been through the wash several hundred times and barely suggested the color blue. A red shirt,
rolled up at the sleeves. Brown cowboy boots walking up
our sidewalk. I couldn't take my eyes off him. I could feel
the neighbors crowding their windows, sizing him up. If
he'd had on a Stetson they could have said "cowboy" to
themselves and been satisfied. But he didn't have a hat, and
his hair was a little on the long side. And did cowboys have
beards? They wouldn't think so. Rappahannock, Virginia,
in 1963, had never seen the likes. Even the Greyhound bus
that stopped on Tuesdays on the way to The Endless Ca-
verns in Luray to let the passengers off to buy soft drinks
and use the rest room at Delbert's General Store had never
seen anything like him. He was compelling, even exotic,
and he was coming right up to my front door.

I had my Rolleiflex camera with me, as always, the one
my mother had given me the year before on my fifteenth
birthday. I don't know what possessed me — maybe it was
to cover my eyes, my shameless stare — but I held the cam-

era steady, focused as he walked into the frame. He stopped. I released the shutter. I breathed again, but just barely.

His teeth were mostly straight and white inside the beard. His eyes were darker than blue — nearly violet, the kind of eyes you could get caught in and stay in with just a single glance.

"*I* know *you*," he said. He smiled, at least that's what I think he did, when he spoke.

It was eerie: this stranger knowing me, staring at me as if he could look through to the other side of me and know everything I was thinking.

"But I don't know *you*."

"Yes you do. You've just forgotten." I waited for him to remind me. That's when he really smiled. It was as if he shared some private joke with himself and wanted to take his time to let me in on it.

My father's footsteps coming down the hall — that's what we both heard — soft thuds as long as the rug lasted, then clomping on the bare floor.

"Jack," my father said. "Jack," he said again, and the word caught in his throat.

Then I knew he was the person my father had called a week ago. I remember my father's vehement whisper into the phone, "I've never asked you for anything — I'm asking you now. Please come here — I need to talk to you."

"So where's Auralee?" Jack said now, looking past him into the house.

My father came out and stood on the porch, but he made no move to shake Jack's hand. His face drained of

color. I waited for him to introduce me, but he acted as if
he'd forgotten I was there.

"Auralee?" my father said. Just hearing her name made
my heart catch — a name I'd never called her. It sounded so
beautiful, but it pained me to hear it then.

"She's gone," my father said.

"I knew it. I just knew it," Jack said, as if he'd been bet-
ting on it, and leaned against the railing, the weariness of
the long drive finally catching up with him. What did he
know, I wondered, and why did he suddenly seem so sad?
How had he even known her?

I stared at him, waiting for him to say what everyone
else had said — "I'm so sorry," or to say nothing and take
our hands. I wanted him to be someone we could welcome, or at least someone who could take our minds off of
things. My first impression of him had been that he was
strong, determined, and strange in a hypnotic, intoxicating
way. Now he looked tired, not like anyone who could save
us from anything.

My father looked as if he wished Jack would just walk
over and embrace him instead of taking up the whole porch
with his weary presence. Jack looked at him, more out of
curiosity than anything else, and played out a long thread of
silence. My father twisted on the very end of it. How in the
world did they know each other? They didn't seem to like
each other at all.

"Oh God, Jack. Jesus Christ." My father's shoulders
began to shake. I was terrified he might cry.

I went to him. "Hey," I said, reminding him I was there.

I searched his face, touched his hand. I looked at Jack. "Why did you come here?"

"He asked me to come," Jack said.

"What for? There's nothing you can do," I said.

Jack looked at my father. "He never told you, did he?" Jack looked away from me, his mouth pressed into a hard line.

I didn't know what it would mean to agree, or disagree. Moving my head in either direction was suddenly impossible.

"He asked me to come," Jack repeated, staring hard at my father.

My normally articulate father remained mute. I waited for him to speak. He didn't. Or couldn't. I began to lose faith that he had the power to, but he finally did.

"I don't expect you to understand." I couldn't tell if he was speaking to Jack or to me. "I've done things in my life I can hardly believe."

"What do you mean?" I said. I tried to keep my voice calm but it rose with every question. "How do you know him? Who *is* he?"

My father left us standing there. He'd said all he was going to say. I called after him as he walked down the hall. "What are we supposed to do now?"

He turned slowly around, silhouetted in the dim hall-way by a lamp on the telephone table behind him. It seemed he had something else to say, but he only stood there, a dark outline, the light weak behind him.

"Matty Louise," Jack whispered. I felt his hand come lightly to the top of my head. No one knew my middle name — it wasn't even on my birth certificate. My mother had given it to me when I was five because I'd liked the name and wanted it for my own.

"Matty Louise, you're my sister." He was using my name like a charm — the proof that he was who he said he was, that he already knew me in ways I didn't understand. The word sister had never been said to me before. Part of me refused to believe it. But something deep down felt it was true.

My father was going. The guard was changing. This new brother, if that's what he was, was all I had left, and he didn't even know me, just my name. In that moment all I knew, and it was like a premonition, was that I could have no secrets from him; they would come spilling out of me, uncontainable, and there was nothing about me he couldn't know if he asked. The thought that he might not want to know never even entered my mind.

ella is nowhere to be seen. Her chair is empty, though it holds an imprint of where she sat earlier, where she's probably been sitting every night for the past twenty years. The door to her room is closed.

There's a blanket over me — she must have put it there before she went to bed. My neck is stiff, my foot still sore. But I can walk. I limp to the truck, and, so as not to wake her, release the brake and let it roll all the way down the hill.

I fall into bed, too tired now to sleep, and haunt myself with images — not those I have taken with a camera, but the ones that have taken me by surprise.

The image I would like to forget is the one of my father just before he left, when he thought he was the only one awake that night. He stood inside the closet that held my mother's clothes, touching the sleeve of her robe as if it still retained her heat. He buried his face in the limp chenille for the last of her scent. Then he started pulling his shirts off hangers one by one until the hangers clanged wildly against one

another. I watched through a crack in the door as he packed
his suitcase.

He turned, and seeing me framed in the doorway he
stared at me, as if I were a painting that had just blinked an
eye. He studied me hard.

Hardly above a whisper, he said, "You're exactly like
her." His face was a caricature of shock, like someone from
a primitive culture who sees his image in a shard of mirror
for the first time and believes it is another, not himself,
trapped inside the glass.

"No," I said. "Like you. I'm exactly like you." I stood
there and waited, knowing my silence, more than any question I had, would force him to speak.

He pushed the halves of the suitcase together until they
clicked. "Then you should understand," he said.

He moved across the room and reached out to me in the
doorway. He stood there with his arms slightly raised, at
half-mast, a small gesture asking for a small response that
would not break either of us. I stood there and let him feel
that empty space between us. His arms started to lower —
he'd accepted the distance that fast. And then I couldn't
stand it anymore. I stepped forward, to let him put his arms
around me the way he'd only a moment ago wanted to. His
arms felt not like a father's but like a boy's, awkward at his
first dance. I knew he wasn't coming back, that he'd held on
much longer than he thought he would. Every day of the
past week I knew he had been waiting for the time when he
could leave, and I couldn't help but think that somehow it
was Jack who'd finally given him permission to go. I wanted to ask him about Jack, but right then I didn't want to

think about this other "family," whether he'd even been married before or not. There wasn't time to explain any of it.

I can no longer remember his last few minutes in that house — how he walked past me — at what speed. Reluctant? Urgent? I cannot recall how I got myself into my own room. There is a blankness around his leaving, a place inside of which something needed to be said, but wasn't. I didn't dare ask him to stay because I knew he would have to say no.

I heard the Studebaker back out of the driveway. It was still mostly dark, but a hint of light started up in the east. I pushed the curtains back. I watched the car stop, its headlights two long funnels across the unmowed lawn. He must have been just sitting there staring, his foot on the brake, because I could see the red light flaring behind. I felt my father lean against the wheel, take a long look, hesitate as he watched the house — the lower half brightly lit, the second-story bedrooms reaching upward into the dark. I opened my window. I swung my legs over the sill. I knew I couldn't stop him, but I thought if I could at least get my feet into the light he would see me. I stretched but couldn't reach. As he backed the rest of the way, I watched the level of light on the house move lower, like water creeping down a drain. He turned into the street, the lights swung across the yard, and I felt a level of dark rising in me like a drug, traveling instantly to every part of me. Then I couldn't feel a thing. I climbed back through the window, though I don't remember the motion or the feel of the wood floor as my feet came back into the room. I forgot the descent down-

stairs — did I hold the handrail or did I crawl on my hands
and knees? At least when I ran away, I didn't make him
watch. I could feel him, as if it were his own footsteps on
that night I had left him, leading me now in a stumbling
lurch through a suddenly empty house. The first thing I felt
was the wool blanket draped across the back of the sofa.
Texture both soft and scratchy. It smelled like dry grass and
lanolin and something else I couldn't name. I rolled myself
in it like a person on fire.

Out of the corner of my eye I saw Jack at the top of the
stairs. I made my way over to the bottom, still wrapped in
the blanket.

His shadow moved — forward or back, I couldn't say; he
was that indistinct.

"Now you know how it feels — to have your father walk
out the door." A piercing chill went through me as if I'd
plunged through a hole in the ice to the black, thick water
below. I felt myself barely held in place by the blanket. If I
moved a muscle I would drop down and down; there would
be no end to it. My voice would never be loud enough to
break the water's surface, to form words that would be carried and heard in the air and light. I fought my way back up.
He was the last person on the surface of the world who
could grab my hand, get me back to shore.

It was as if he'd read my mind or was somehow inside
my skin — he knew me that well. I felt him shiver where he
stood. I could not believe my eyes even though they'd
become so accustomed to the dark, when he came out of
nowhere, down those twenty-three stairs, out of the storm-
gray air and drew me to him. He put his arms around my

wrapped form, wound tight inside the wool winding sheet. He held me close in a way I'd never been held, near and far, soothed and scared at the same time. Armless, legless, I could not hold him back. But I felt the compelling contradiction — the downward pull of loneliness in the midst of someone's arms.

He stepped away from me more slowly than he'd come forward, and I thought I felt him hesitate, as if he'd come so far and rehearsed his lines so long for this particular scene that he was reluctant for it to be over with so quickly.

I stood motionless, taller than I'd ever been and infinitely more contained. I felt a sinking dread that I would never be able to get clear of this night, these sounds, these images, the feel of being held by him — gathered together for half a minute I would never be able to forget, afraid I couldn't rest until I had all of him.

Jack stayed, at least for a while, and I'm not sure if he was bound by duty, some promise made to our father, or if we were binding ourselves together out of common loss. Even so, every day he was there I worried it was his last, that as soon as he'd fulfilled his obligation he'd go back to his own life again. About his origins he would only say that my father had been married to his mother until he met mine. I'm sure I had at least a hundred questions, all of them jammed up, waiting for the least little opening from him. He kept closed, a brother in name only. There was no story to put him in.

Jack joined a state highway crew to repair the bridge the Rappahannock River had washed out in a freak storm, and the whole town prospered briefly from the damage. I made Jack's lunch every morning along with my own, and we sat at the kitchen table like every other couple in the county, drinking coffee mixed with chicory and listening to the morning news on the radio. I did everything a wife would do except kiss him good-bye and make love to him in that last dreamy weariness before he fell asleep.

He always cooked supper — spaghetti and stews and things that simmered for hours in pots. That's what I remember most about that time. He never measured anything, and he never let me help. He had his own way of doing things, he said.

One day, the bridge was finished, and Mr. Harlan, the postmaster, was the first to drive across. Reverend Payne cut the ribbon donated by the general store, and the whole town applauded wildly as Mr. Harlan's old De Soto rolled over the new pine boards. He stopped midway, and we all held our breath. He got out of the car and tested the bridge himself — flexed his knees like someone on a diving board. He turned back toward us and waved. It held. No one doubted that it would, but there was something breathtaking about that moment, as if we were all there to witness an act of extraordinary faith at the impossibility of something as heavy as a car held in the air by a mere wooden bridge.

There was a picnic afterward on the church lawn. A phalanx of Episcopalian women presided over the card tables piled with Smithfield ham and green beans and rolls. Jack and the rest of the men gathered around a horseshoe pitch, gripping cans of Black Label beer as they waited their turn.

I watched him throw. I felt awkward among the women, preparing food for the men, shut out of the game and left to cheer on the sidelines. When the game ended, Jack drifted over to the tables. I held a forkful of Mrs. Timberlake's chess pie for him to eat. He opened his mouth wide and swallowed, then gave an appreciative groan.

My friend since the fifth grade, Carolyn McCormick, was serving coffee at the next table. I hadn't seen her since the funeral, and when I looked at her holding out paper cups, dressed in a pink flowered dress and strappy pink sandals and toenails to match, I knew she had crossed over, become one of them, the ladies who presided, who watched and gossiped and condemned anyone who strayed too far beyond the lines.

Carolyn looked at me sharply, as if I were making a colossal fool out of myself and would be the last one to know it.

I couldn't tell anyone, not even her, that I was holding out the hope that Jack would make things right, that he would claim me — move in permanently or take me with him when he left.

But the day came when he said he had to go soon and there was no mention of my coming with him. He said he'd taken care of all the arrangements to have me board with Mrs. Timberlake, the church organist. The house and most of the things in it would be sold to pay the past due on the mortgage.

Part of me believed him; the other half held defiantly to the idea that he wouldn't leave me. I was desperate to solidify things, make a mark, an impression; and after I did, he could leave, but he wouldn't be long in Arizona before he'd call and ask me to come to live with him.

I made Jack drive me to Winchester, to the county fair, on his last weekend. We parked in a lopsided row in a lumpy field, and as we walked to the fairgrounds I put my arm through his. We strolled through the sawdust-strewn aisles that wound through the game booths, my long-legged stride easily matching his own.

"Come on — win a prize for your sweetheart." A boy no older than me held out a bunch of small wooden hoops — bangles to toss around the lips of fishbowls. "Come on," the boy teased. "She'll love you a lot if you win." He sucked on an unfiltered cigarette. A hank of greasy hair hung in his eyes. I felt suddenly shy, afraid to look at Jack. I waited for him to say "She's not my girl," but he didn't. Maybe he didn't think it was worth the bother. He took the hoops from the boy, narrowed his eyes in concentration as he took aim, and let fly. The first one glanced off the bowl with a sharp ping, and the two goldfish darted crazily inside their small see-through world. The second one hit the mark, then slipped. The third one clattered onto the wooden shelf between the second and third tiers. The boy eyed me and folded his arms. Everything about him smirked.

The fourth one found its mark, and settled like a lid on a jar. The goldfish flinched when it landed but quickly re-sumed their suspended pose. The last hoop was true also, and landed on a bowl that contained just one swimming fish — the other floated like an oyster cracker on the sur-face.

The boy retrieved the hoops reluctantly, spotting the dead fish. "Well, shit now," he said. "That's the third one today. The water must be no good around here." He scooped it out with a tea strainer and tossed it in a coffee can. He turned to face us. "Which one you want — you got a choice — anything on that first row there." He pointed to a shelf lined with small stuffed animals, beer mugs, colored-glass ashtrays.

"Which one do you want?" Jack asked me.

I scanned the shelf. None of it was very appealing. But at the end of the row there was a small, gray elephant made of metal with a red felt saddle and golden tassels.

"I want that," I said, pointing to it.

"This?" the boy said, touching his fingers to a blond-haired plastic doll next to it.

"No — that," I said, waving my hand impatiently to the right. He moved his fingers until they closed on the elephant, and I almost couldn't bear for him to touch it. His fingers looked dirty, mean.

"This? You want *this?*" he asked. "Nobody's ever wanted one of these. The dolls are popular. The ashtrays, too."

"Well that's what I want."

"Then that's what you get," he said. I couldn't tell if he thought I was weird or just stupid. He didn't seem to think it was much of a prize. He planted it on the counter. Two gold tassels hanging from the red saddle quivered.

Jack nodded. "That's the only good thing here."

We waded into the moving throng. I glanced behind me once and saw the boy scoop a new goldfish out of a plastic bag and toss it in to join the single fish.

"When you were little, maybe four or five, you rode an elephant at the Bronx Zoo," Jack said.

"How do you know about that?" I remembered the zoo, but not the elephant ride. He stopped at another booth, laid fifty cents on the counter, and scooped up three ragged softballs.

"I was there — it was on your birthday. I watched you ride. I was too scared to go with you. And mad, too, that you showed up at all." He looked at the target of wooden bottles, not at me. He threw all three balls but only knocked over the top bottle on a tier.

"What were you doing there? Who did I think you were?"

"I have no idea. Probably just some kid who came along. Your mom was there. She knew. You all were passing through — I think it was her idea to have him call me and invite me along. It was only for an afternoon."

"What happened to your mom?" I asked.

"He dumped her for yours. I already told you."

With the last of a second set of softballs, he smashed the two bottles. "She died — ten years ago, of a stroke. I called him to tell him. He said he would come. He never did." He threw a couple more softballs; only the last one hit, not enough to win a prize, just a free turn, which he gave away to the next person in line. We walked slowly down the midway. I tried to imagine Jack watching me climb onto an enormous animal, leaving him on the ground. I wished I had known who he was. It bothered me to think of him on the ground, a boy stubbornly rooted, outshone by his sister. I tried to picture myself as I rode away from him — a little girl astride a gray mountain, unafraid. For the second

time since he'd come to Virginia I felt his other side —
something subterranean and unforgiving.

"Did you hate me then?" I asked. It occurred to me that
he still might. I stopped dead in my tracks to face him. I
needed to see his eyes.

"Some," he said. He looked at me a little helplessly; then
he started walking again. "No, not a little. A lot." He
wouldn't look at me, even when I planted myself square in
front of him. "It doesn't matter now." He took a step back,
then walked around me.

I could hear a bluegrass band playing a waltz from a
makeshift stage strung with colored light bulbs. I thought it
might help if we danced — it was a way to get close again,
with music as the perfect excuse. I didn't think Jack would
ask me to, so I asked him to dance. At first he said no, but I
pulled him by the hand into the crowd, and we got caught
up in the current of everybody else's waltz.

I could smell his sweat and a little of the soap he'd used
that morning. I could feel his resistance in every step he
took, as if his real self were pinned in place back on the sidelines and I was stretching him near to breaking.

We danced one dance, then just stood and watched
everybody else until the band packed up. We moved slowly
into the dark field toward the parked cars and trucks, following other people's flashlights. We drove slowly to the
gate in a long line of cars trundling slowly through the dust,
evacuating the folding-up fair, heading back to a more permanent world.

On the ride home I pretended to fall asleep, let my head
rest on his shoulder. I closed my eyes, felt the headlights of
oncoming cars sweep across my face. I felt the bones in

Jack's shoulder move as he shifted down for the hills. I wondered if he would put his arm around me like my father
used to, letting me work the gears with my left hand while
he worked the clutch. But he didn't, and when we hit a pothole and my head bounced away from him, I didn't lean
against him again.

We pulled into the driveway. He cut the engine. I still
didn't move. I waited for him to say, "Matty, wake up, we're
home," which he did, and I rubbed my eyes as if he'd called
me back from a dream.

We trudged up the steps, then said good night in the hall
like guests who've stayed a long time in the same hotel and
begin to know each other's habits, guests who greet each
other outside the doors but will never know the inside of
each other's rooms.

The next night Jack stood in the kitchen grating parmesan for our last spaghetti dinner.

"Can't you just stay?" I heard the edge in my voice, but
I'm not sure he did.

"This isn't my home," he said quietly. I knew he had his
own life, that he had to go. I was the one that didn't have
one. I wanted him to stop what he was doing — really, the
mundaneness of the cheese grating was infuriating. I
knocked it from his hand and it fell with a clatter to the
floor; immediately I hated that my hand had just done what
it wanted without my say-so. I was not a girl he could love.
I was a child in the midst of a tantrum.

I ran out the back door, across the yard to the weather-
darkened scaffolding of a treehouse my father had started
ten years before and never finished. I climbed the ladder

that had leaned so long against the tree it had become a part of it. Branches snaked their way through the rungs. I took the rusty hammer lying on the platform floor. I held it tightly and felt the hammer slowly rise toward the culmination of an action I'd always wanted to take. I began to strike at the nearest two-by-four with the claw end. The sound of metal on wood rang through the dark. I thought I saw Jack's shape in the window of my father's room. I swung harder. I wanted him to watch, thought if I swung hard enough he would feel the blows like an aftershock that would follow him across every state line he had to cross, every mile he was about to put between us.

I was hell-bent on pulling it all down with my bare hands if I had to. It didn't take long enough. I shook with adrenaline that had been summoned for fight or flight, and so little had been used. I stood there in the splintered mess wishing there had been entire walls, a ceiling to destroy.

If Jack were watching, he didn't do it for long. He came to me with a toolbox, set it down and opened it. I stopped what I was doing and stared. He took out a jar of nails, unscrewed the lid.

"Use the other end," he said, nodding at the hammer. He handed me some nails.

I couldn't. I stood there, too furious to speak. He didn't say another word, just grabbed a plank off the pile my father had left to rot and started to nail it into place. By the time he was on his third plank, a room was forming and I began to imagine the rest. I wanted it badly — a wall, an actual roof, a finish to the thing.

It must have been close to midnight when we got done.

The treehouse looked lopsided, but the platform held my weight.

"You've pounded the shit out of these nails," he said. "Now get some sleep."

I stayed awake a long time, pacing in my room. I wanted to feel the entire length of him wrapped around me. I waited at least an hour until I was sure he was asleep, and then I tiptoed across the hall.

His breathing was measured, heavy. I stood there — I don't know how long — just listening to it. He didn't move a muscle — that's how deeply he slept. I lifted the covers so slowly I was aware of each bone in my hand bending, the tendons slowly flexing to the task. I slipped in beside him. He didn't wake, didn't even stir. He was sleeping on his side, facing away from me. I lay there on my back, rigid, my heart beating so hard it shook my body as if begging me to let it out. I shifted my weight by degrees until I was lying on my side. I was moving in slow motion, and it was excruciating because I was so terribly frightened. I knew I should get out now, but I'd already gone over the line. I slid my arm across his chest and curved my body into his. A sound came from him — a little groan. He pulled my arm closer around him and curled his hand around mine. "Jack," I whispered. He didn't answer. His breathing went back to its deep cadence. His mind was far away in a dream, but his body knew another body was near. I stayed there, matching my breathing to his, but I was wide awake. My mind wanted my hand to uncurl from his, to find its way down his chest, his stomach, stroke his genitals, his thighs. My hand stayed where it was. But in my mind I did all these things and more. When the light went from black to gray I slipped away from him, out from under the covers, out of his bed, out of his room, back to my own where I watched the sun rise to make sure it still would. I was so aroused and ashamed I thought that God, who had never paid attention to me, would punish me with a night so endless I would beg forgiveness just to have the sun again. The sun came up and the birds sang as they always did, hopefully, continually, whether another answered or not.

In an hour or so, Jack would be leaving. The truck would head down the street in the opposite direction from which it first came. I didn't think I could bear to watch it go, and in the end I didn't. I said good-bye on the porch, then went back into the house and straight out the back door as soon as the engine started up. I sat in my treehouse, hugging my knees.

I began to want what my father had, what he had probably already passed on to me — a certain kind of love that, like a wild river, would jump its banks, work its way around trees and rocks, houses if it had to, to find itself an ocean.

I climbed the narrow stairs to my attic room, to my perch above the town. I'd been living in Mrs. Timberlake's house for two weeks since my father left, since Jack had come and gone. I tried, from that vantage point, to feel the directions everyone had taken — my mother straight up and skyward; my father, south, I imagined, to the New Orleans of his vagabond days where he'd first met her; Jack, due west, back to the Arizona he'd materialized from.

I always knew my father was going to leave and maybe

even leave the way he did, although that's not the story he used to tell me. When I turned eighteen and could legally go — no more running away, he said — when that day came, he would go too, back to New Orleans, as if he could pick up on the life of the poet he'd left behind thirty-five years ago, as if that life were still waiting to be resumed. But the big surprise was that he'd beat me to it. I'd been holding out for that eighteenth birthday for his sake and now he was gone. I had my itinerary, a map of California with a red pin stuck in San Francisco, and just six months shy of my liberation day he leaves town. Maybe he couldn't stand the thought of being left again, so he jumped the gun.

I looked out my attic window, my first home away from home, just down the street from the old one. The people of Rappahannock had done their duty, had ensconced me as Mrs. Timberlake's gal Friday, her seeing-eye dog, until I came of age. Glaucoma had recently taken much of her tenuous sight. She said I was a godsend. I believe now that if she could have seen me clearly then she'd know that the devil had taken my idle, fidgeting hands and given them something dark to do. We were living at opposite ends of the house — I was at the apex, she on the ground floor. Every night she heard my footsteps on the stairs whose undersides comprised part of her slanted ceiling. I would take them two at a time while she stayed below, unable to navigate even the first of the two flights anymore.

From the window, I watched the congregation that had temporary collective control over my life slowly leak out of the white container of the church and spread out across the lawn. If I'd been the nine-year-old tomboy I used to be, I would have aimed a peashooter, picked them off one by one. But I had no shooter, just the sharp, constant pinch of adolescent resentment. Five months longer and I would be eighteen, and no one could stop me from leaving, too. I'd have an ID that would keep me from being picked up by the police, that would make me a free agent in the world outside of Virginia.

I leaned my elbows on the sun-warped sill and stared. This was the day that the furniture I had sat and slept on all my life, the dishes I had eaten from and washed and dried and once in a while broken in sudden anger would be revealed in broad daylight in the yard down the street — rummaged through and sold so the bank could get back its past due, now going into ninety days.

I became a camera, constantly aimed, catching people unaware, recording the fixtures, the details of my life being carried away.

Cletus, the church janitor, and Reverend Payne himself carried what was once my mattress into the yard. Even from the height of my attic window I could see the stigmata of my first menstruation, now a permanent rust-colored Rorschach blot on the blue-and-white-striped ticking. They leaned the mattress against a dogwood tree, but Reverend Payne, as he stepped back, must have seen it because he stepped forward again quickly and turned the mattress over. Perhaps he feared it was the telltale emblem of my deflowering. But that had happened in a young girl's room in New Jersey, and there had not been enough blood to leave a permanent stain. I never told a soul. All I'd heard for years was a lecture on virginity from my father, about

saving it — not for anything so vague as respect from boys
who supposedly had to have it as proof of purity, but as
something truly mine that could be withheld, as if to give it
was the same as Samson willingly shearing off his own hair.
I always wondered what my mother, had she lived, would
have said about the consequences of sex — that it was not
merely risky, but fatal, and forever?

Women came from the propped-open door of the house
bearing pots and pans, as if in preparation for a banquet.
But there was nothing in those pots except the odd bit of
dust, the small curled carcass of a spider. My friend Carolyn
lined up rows of shoes on the lawn. My mother's red high
heels — her tango shoes, she'd called them — tilted in the
grass. As I watched, one red shoe fell over, surrendered
itself to the bright, green grass, and nobody stooped to set
it right again.

An armoire mirror came next — flashed the sun straight
into my eyes. It fitfully caught the yard and a woman holding my mother's green silk dress against her body to see if it
suited her before the mirror was leaned against a chestnut
tree. The image it reflected back then — branches mostly
and blue pieces of sky — held steady.

People came to buy slowly, hesitantly, as if my father
might drive up in a furious cloud of sprayed gravel and send
them all away. After a while, they moved in closer. I
watched people inspect our belongings — lift the lids on
pots and pans, work the egg beater, test my parents' bed,
and make off with these things down the street in their
arms if they could carry them, in the trunks of their cars or
their pickups if they couldn't. After that, whenever I visited

people, I would find these things in their living rooms and kitchens. Mr. Turner had my father's trunk in his front hall-way, and in Mrs. Catlett's pantry I once saw the china my mother had ordered all the way from England. Even Mrs. Timberlake had bought something — my mother's seed pearls coiled in a pink satin box. The clasp was broken, which pleased me. Mrs. Timberlake never did get around to fixing it, so I didn't have to look at a young woman's necklace on the wrinkled, freckled folds of someone else's skin. Even so, the first time I saw it when I was dusting in her room I broke down and cried, then I pulled off the beads one by one, a kind of vengeful counting of a rosary. By the last pale bead, my tears were done.

What things I had left fit in my angular room under the eaves: a cane chair that had belonged to my great-grand-father Elijah who'd fought in the Civil War, a box of photo-graphs and the family album they were never pasted into, some books of Irish poetry, my mother's Bible full of pressed flowers picked every summer of her life.

That night, after the yard sale was over, felt endless. I couldn't sleep because I heard each and every night noise as separate, amplified — the shriek of tree frogs just outside my window, an owl, fussing its wings, coming in and out of a hole just beneath the eaves, and the roof crackling inter-mittently as the house cooled down, slowly exhaling its stored-up June heat.

I went to the window. I looked down the street at the house I used to live in. There was a single light in my old bedroom, and it went off as I watched. The new owners had already arrived and were walking through the empty

rooms deciding what would go where. I shoved the bed
beneath the window and lay with my head tilted back to
see the stars. I took off my nightgown. It was almost like
sleeping outside, feeling the breeze trace across my skin.
For the first time in my attic room I began the ceremony I'd
performed every night of my life since my body had been
taken so violently by a total stranger. I was taking it back. I
was teaching my body a new idea of love, superimposing
tenderness over the dirty, crying shame. I lay perfectly still.
I did not move. I did not touch myself. In my mind I had a
lover whose face was always hidden to me, who touched
me as if he knew every bone and tendon by heart.

As I lay there halfway dreaming, I wondered if the dead
got confused, tried to find their children through windows
where they last saw them, not understanding that they've
moved away. I felt my mother draw near. The moon
showed itself through the tree's black branches; I let her
look at me as long as she wanted. I wondered what she saw,
if the naked body of a full-grown daughter was something
she could believe had once come from her own.

Jack's features came slowly to light like a face emerging
from a dream. I lifted the paper from the developer tray
until it was just inches from my face, and I sent my breath
toward an overexposed place on his cheek so the heat
would hurry it, darken it. I put the photograph back in the
chemistry.

I stood alone in a tiny basement room bathed in red
light. Before me, a white piece of paper floated in a tray. I
held the tray with both hands, rocked it gently to keep the

developer contained, created a minor disturbance in a small body of water — enough to coax the face straight out of emulsion. The hair and beard, because they were darkest, came first. The pupils next. He continued to rise like a drowned face surfacing in a lake. Still, he would only come so far; still, he was divided. I loved his face from the first minute I saw him. What I wanted was to hold that face in my hands — the actual flesh, not the piece of paper that represented him. I wouldn't be struck down by the gods. They'd taken all they were going to get from me.

Above me, the church floor shook as the congregation rose to its feet, and the bass notes of the organ, which began in Mrs. Timberlake's arthritic hands, trembled the planks of the floor. A muffled hymn began, wavering toward praise. Let them look up in the rafters, I thought, for a glimpse of God. I looked down at the picture I'd created — a graven image, Reverend Payne might say, though he himself had given me the darkroom tools for what he thought would become a hobby but what instead was becoming an obsession. This was the only way he could get me inside the church, since I refused to come through the front door. I had no faith for it anymore. My mother had finally summoned my father — or so it seemed to me — not to any address on earth but to a vague set of coordinates in the ever-after. My father heard only the lost music of her voice calling from an unlocatable source, a constantly changing river that he could not in this life hope to cross. But like Orpheus, he thought love could bring her back, and so he had set out after her. Somebody always had to be leaving, somebody left behind. That's what I told myself.

The left-behind always need a story, and this was becoming mine.

The congregation sank heavily into their pews. I could not hear the words, but I knew from the rhythm, from the length of the sentences, that they were responding to Reverend Payne — "The Lord be with you. And with thy spirit. Let us pray." A long silence settled above me. The sermon began when the floor creaked only intermittently, punctuating the endless minutes of the better part of an hour.

Jack's face held back his features, refusing to be fully revealed. I switched on the light, like Psyche holding the lamp to Eros's sleeping form, and for a few seconds had the satisfaction of watching his face react. His features flooded in until, with the same speed he had driven away from me, he clouded over completely and left a piece of paper behind as black and incomprehensible as the Book of Common Prayer.

I poured the chemicals back in their brown glass bottles, washed the trays and turned them over to drain in the trough that served as my darkroom sink. I left the church basement before the service ended and could still hear Reverend Payne's voice pleading with his flock. It seemed to me they indulged him as he strained to translate the voice of God. I could feel their distracted gazes through the stained glass follow me across the churchyard, could feel how they envied my freedom at least as much as they pitied it as I moved through the just-cut grass, in the moving air, the benevolent light. "Poor child," I could almost hear them thinking. There was not one among them who would have said I was blessed. I was outside the circle of society, where things made sense. I was closer to what might be called cursed, but I was finally what I'd always wanted to be: one of a kind, beyond recrimination or reprimand or even advice. If they had any of that, they held it back; none of it applied to me anymore.

From my attic window I watched the thick, humid haze settle over the town as the sun went behind the mountains. I could see the porch door on Delbert Rider's store open and close for its Saturday customers. I could see my old house and watched a man carry things inside it — boxes, an old refrigerator, a couch, two beds — one double, one single. From that distance, things had a pattern, and I wanted to fix it in my mind forever. I took aim through the lens. I shot it all, a frame at a time. Nothing escaped me.

I saw Carolyn come out of Delbert's store with a paper sack of groceries. Once my closest friend, she was no longer on my side. We'd formed a "girl gang" in the fifth grade, with ourselves as the sole members. We initiated each other with petty theft from the five-and-dime, sneaking out of our respective houses at night to perform some ritual vandalism. Once we walked down the road at midnight to the Black church and threw a rock in the window, for no particular reason other than at that age we'd picked up some of the ignorance and fear that surrounded us. Our schools were completely segregated, the county holding out for pressure from the federal government before they integrated. It would be several years before that happened, and when it did Carolyn and I had our first parting of the ways. Integration began in our class with the introduction of a single black boy from Central Elementary. His name was Otis and I liked him immediately. He was a natural storyteller and made up fantastic tales about animals that talked and took over the world. Carolyn thought he was retarded, which, in a sixth grader's mind, is worse than being a different color.

Boundaries all around us shifted; new lines were drawn between black and white. My friendship with Carolyn began its own redefinition. When my mother got sick the first time, before she actually went into the hospital, it seemed that the premonition of grief began to divide Carolyn and me. We decided to become blood sisters. At the time it seemed the natural evolution of our friendship, but now when I remember it, it seems we were grasping at straws, that it was a last-ditch attempt to stay together. We pricked our fingers and wrote our names with a crow quill dipped in mingled blood. We buried the paper we wrote our names on in a Roi-Tan cigar box along with a wooden cross pendant I snitched from the choir room at the church, a coal-black marble that was magnetized, and the wing bones of a cardinal that had broken its neck when it flew into the living room window. But two years later, after the funeral, when Carolyn asked, "Aren't you ever going to cry?" she looked afraid of me, as if the absence of tears had made me dangerous, capable of something as terrible and powerful as murder or suicide. That day I went straight to the spot beneath the dogwood tree where we'd buried the cigar box. Because of the shallowness of the hole and the recent heavy rains the box had given up its shape, had become so much a part of the earth that held it that the only thing I could find for sure in the mulch was the black marble, which, once lustrous, mysterious in its ability to draw iron filings and paper clips from inches away, was now dirt-dulled and powerless. The paper with our names on it had dissolved.

When I watched Carolyn come out of Delbert's store, she looked so small, diminished, the size she had been when we were close. From my perspective she looked like the girl whose finger shook when she touched it to mine, and I could hardly remember the beads of blood we had each provoked from ourselves as a gift, a pact that was supposed to bind us forever.

From the window I took her picture and reduced her to the size of a child against the wide road and tall trees of town. I wasn't going to, but I found myself calling to her. She stopped, halfway across the road, looked around, unable to locate my voice. Then she looked up. She stared up at me and I felt as if I'd flown inside her and was looking out and up at myself, a girl in a window, Rapunzel without a braid. Before I could stop myself, I beckoned to her to come up. She nodded and walked out of my field of vision. I heard her footsteps on the porch, her timid knock. I shouted down three flights for her to come in, and with each step that brought her closer I felt a wildfire panic — as soon as she stepped into my room she would see how a lifetime of living in all those houses had been shrunk down to a cubbyhole beneath the eaves.

Carolyn ducked her head through the tiny doorway, set the groceries down. She scanned the room before she looked at me. "How long do you have to stay here?" she asked, not bothering with her usually flawless southern manners.

"It's temporary," I said quickly.

"Six months until your birthday   that's not too bad."

I found myself smiling, pleased that she remembered, that there was something in my life that hadn't changed. She turned her gaze from me to the photographs covering the walls. "That's him, isn't it — that stepbrother or whatever he was. I had no idea you had one."

"Neither did I," I said and felt that old pull of complicity, that the next thing we would do was sit right down cross-legged on the floor and whisper halfway through the night. "He's my *half*-brother. We have the same father."

"Oh," she said, as if that explained everything, or nothing, as if it would have been better to have the other parent in common.

She continued to scan the photographs. I'd duplicated the only one I'd taken of him in eleven different exposures, one right after the other, from blank white to pitch black and all the deepening grays in between.

She turned toward me. I imagined I could hear the pivoting joints inside her knees. "Look at this. You'd think he was your boyfriend."

I flushed dark with an embarrassment I didn't know I had. It was like being told I was a sleepwalker and did unspeakable things in the night. I simply had no idea how other people saw anything that had to do with me anymore, and yet now it was clear — because even I could see it — I'd stolen his image, if not his very soul, and turned it into a fetish.

"He's my *brother!*" I wanted to say with indignation, but it came out more like an alibi.

"You said half," she countered, which was an accurate but somehow shameful fact, as if he'd only partly succeeded.

She didn't accuse me, really, but still I felt I'd been found out. Photographs could work against you — evidence, proof, subject to all kinds of interpretations. People could walk into your room and by seeing what you put on your walls could read you like a book, cover to cover, in less than a minute flat.

"You know what I think, Matty? You need to fall in love. It takes your mind off all kinds of things. Here." She reached inside her purse and took out an envelope, handed it to me. Carolyn crossed her legs. "At first I thought I'd die when I flunked out. Don't look so shocked — it was inevitable. I never gave a damn about school, you know that. So I didn't graduate. So what? Now I've got a wedding to plan. It takes up a lot of time. And this is one thing I'm going to succeed at."

I pulled out the invitation — an extravagance of loopy gold script raised from the surface of the paper, not unlike the projects we used to do in the third grade, writing with Elmer's glue and then scattering glitter dust that dried and hardened into shining words.

"You don't know him. I met him at the Gold Cup races last year. He's from Loudon County — his family breeds thoroughbred horses. Anyway, you have to come to the wedding. I'll even aim the bouquet right at you." She gazed up into the rafters, then back at me. "Get yourself a fiancé — then you'll have somewhere to go." She opened up her purse again, took out a ten-dollar bill that was folded up into a neat little square. It was so creased it looked like it would tear. "Here," she said, unfolding it carefully.

"No, I can't. That's your emergency money."

"I'm not going to have an emergency now. Get yourself to the beauty parlor. Look at you."

"Well, I've been buying film — things for the dark-room." I felt ridiculous saying it — one look at the room made it obvious what I spent my money on. It was like I had a habit that constantly needed feeding. She pushed the money in my hand, closed my fingers around it.

"You need to get out of here — all that Beethoven music downstairs and all these pictures up here . . ." She waved her free hand in the air. "It's weird. It doesn't suit you."

It does, though — you just don't see it, I thought.

"Matty, everything has escaped you. Nothing can get to you up here. Nothing."

We stood in the heat-stuffed room. A shine of sweat came through her skin. I thought if she just kept at it she could break me down. She was closer than she knew.

She snapped her purse shut, adjusted the strap on her shoulder before she lifted up the sack of groceries again. I watched her, amazed at the change in her. She had seemed awkward before, even shy. I had always been the one in grade school with schemes and mischief and little plans to break the law. Now, whatever awkwardness used to be in her had coalesced into a single-minded purposefulness. She glanced back at the pictures of Jack and shook her head. "Trouble," she said, as if she were commenting on some-one in a wanted poster on the post office bulletin board.

I looked at the pictures, but I couldn't see it. To me he just looked startled, scared.

I knew I would not buy a dress or go to the beauty parlor, would not go to her wedding. I'd use her money to get out of town.

From my window, I watched her disappear down the street, toward that wedding day she'd decided was the real beginning of her life. I looked at the invitation again, the date November 1. The day before my birthday. Carolyn was getting hitched, and I was going to be home free. This time I wouldn't be leaving by the window in the middle of the night as I did when I was sixteen. This time I'd be walking right out the front door, closing it hard behind me.

Music drifted up the two flights of stairs, drawing me down. Mrs. Timberlake had left the French doors to the music parlor open so what precious little breeze there was could freely enter the room. She had taken on a new piano student, a boy whose family had just moved to town. The only boy I'd known who'd ever taken piano lessons was one in the third grade, Leonard Mateo, who'd spent a year in an iron lung and now went everywhere in a wheelchair, his body from the waist down something he no longer had access to.

I stood in the open doorway and watched the back of the new boy who played so well. His music rolled through the rooms like mist moving low across a lake, as if it loved its source and could not bear to float away completely — Chopin's nocturnes, Debussy's "Clair de Lune." I didn't see a wheelchair, or even a pair of crutches. Blue jeans and a

white T-shirt. Dark hair culminating in a ducktail. All this
was ordinary, but the way he played wasn't. Not just his
hands were involved in playing — his whole body leaned
into the music.

So often in the two weeks since I had been there I had
heard Mrs. Timberlake cry out instructions to her pupils,
but with this boy she was silent. I saw her head nodding in
rhythm and approval, and also, I thought, in gratitude.
When he was finished he laid his hands on his thighs and
seemed to collapse in the aftermath of the nocturne. He
slouched on the stool, looked almost defeated by the
silence. He kept looking at the page, at the notes that still
moved inside his motionless hands.

I stared at his back. His shoulder blades were clearly visible through his shirt because of his slouch. I don't think I
made any sound at all, but he turned his head to the right,
listening, as if some distant music came from another room
and he needed to hear it. He turned all the way around.
The swivel stool creaked. His glasses caught the reflection
of the sunset as his gaze swept past the window, to me.

We looked at each other, a little startled. I wondered if
he knew how long I'd been standing there, listening. Mrs.
Timberlake was oblivious. She was somewhere in Chopin's
Poland. Eventually she came back to us. We still hadn't
moved a muscle, still hung inside that second of recognition
across a room, though we'd never seen each other before in
our lives.

"Oh, Matty!" she cried and laughed nervously, like a
girl, I thought. "This is Benjamin O'Neil — he just moved
into your old house."

My gaze had left him momentarily while she spoke, but when I looked at him again I felt oddly ashamed, as if I had somehow been evicted from my home and was now the lowly serving girl in Mrs. Timberlake's house. I was absolutely certain that he slept in my old room, and I wondered if he'd felt my presence there, like a ghost haunting the last place it lived. But then I remembered that out of defiance or some sense of last-minute claim, I'd left a photograph of myself on the back of the closet door, the camera held above my head, the lens tilted down, aimed at my naked reflection in a full-length mirror. I could feel him putting the images together, and I saw the very moment that happened because he suddenly stared, transfixed, as if he'd just walked in on me as I was slowly pulling a dress over my head of my own free will.

He looked up again. He smiled, in what I took to be a kind of collusion. All I knew was that I had the feeling, from the way he played the music, that he had summoned me. Then again, maybe it was the other way around — the picture of myself on his closet door had brought him to the source, had called him to this house, to me.

The family album, or what passed for one, had been shut up in a box ever since my mother died. I'd been avoiding going through the cartons of odds and ends that Reverend Payne had salvaged from my father's desk after he bought it at the yard sale. Now I pulled it from under my bed. I opened the album, frightened to see her face, but more frightened that I'd forgotten what she looked like, that the way I remembered her was wrong, somehow, that I'd shaped her to fit the idea I had of her — enigmatic, striking, vibrant, and alive. When I opened the book I found my father's theft: the little white corners that had once held her image to the page now held nothing but the ghost of a gray square barely lighter than the black construction paper they had once been affixed to. All that was left were pictures of me and my father that she must have taken — a chronology from birth to age five. There they stopped. It was as if I'd never grown any older, or at least the pictures had no longer been assembled in the album. Maybe they had stuck together in the original processing envelopes or even been thrown away by accident.

In a small cardboard box beneath a pile of cuff links, two dead watches, and a few Mexican pesos, I found a roll of film, exposed but undeveloped. I hardly dared touch it — it was like finding gold, or the next best thing to it. I wanted to run with it to the darkroom, but I made myself slow down, take my time, not only because I was afraid that if I hurried I might accidentally ruin it, but I wanted to delay the possibility of disappointment. It might, after all, be nothing more than vistas from the Blue Ridge Parkway, and if there were pictures of my mother, the film might be unsalvageable, destroyed by who knows how many years of heat and humidity.

As I carefully wound the film around the reel I could sense it through my fingers. She was there. She had to be. I poured the developer in the canister and rocked it gently back and forth, the reel clinking against the stainless steel like Chinese bells. Come on, I said, coaxing her. Be there. Be there. Be there.

I unwound the dark gray film and pulled the long sheet of twelve squares from the reel. Two were blank — completely clear windows. One was unintelligible — a blur of negative shapes — a foot? part of a folding chair? an accidental exposure aimed nowhere. And then there was the shape of her — three successive frames, her body slowly turning to face the camera by degrees. I recognized the setting — the Shenandoah River, the summer we spent there just before she got sick. The negative image of her, so silvery and black, was frightening, as if a fleeting glimpse of her had been taken on the other side, wherever she was. Death had turned her dark hair white, her skin a cool, charcoal gray, her eyes a glittering opalescence, and the river and the trees a haunting lace etched through to bare emulsion.

I did not print these negatives. I couldn't, at least not yet. I knew her face would be innocent of the future that was so much shorter than she would ever have dreamed, and I couldn't bear to see it. I thought it would be a long time before I could look again.

I wondered if the impulse to take a picture of someone was in some way a premonition of their death or disappearance. The image itself becomes timeless. It is not a moment frozen in time, but an eternal present tense. I could not look at a photograph of my mother in the river and say, "In this picture my mother stood in the river." No. In this picture my mother *is standing* in the river. She will always be standing in this river.

That same day I found a picture stuck face down to the back of my mother's baptism certificate in the back of her

Bible. In the picture, two girls lean their heads together, and light shines on their straight dark hair. The older girl, about ten or eleven, has her arm around the younger one, who can't be more than eight or so. Something about the older one draws me — the set of her mouth, the level stare she gives the photographer. It's not the eyes that give her away, but the angle at which she holds her head — a shyness despite the stare, a half-turning, as if she can't wait to be gone.

Even though I had never seen any pictures of my mother when she was a girl, I recognized her. Who is the girl my mother leans her head against? I turned the snapshot over. In faded blue ink, in my grandmother's hand, was written: Emma and Auralee, 1936, Lake Pontchartrain. I looked closely. There was something similar about the eyes, but not strikingly so. They could have been friends.

I took the photo to Mrs. Timberlake. "Who is this girl with my mother?" I asked.

She held it close to her face and peered at it through her thick, rimless glasses. She squinted, then shook her head.

"It says 'Emma' on the back," I told her.

She handed it back to me. "Emma." She shook her head again, then sat down slowly in the wing-backed chair. "Your mother's sister."

My stomach tightened, and the floor suddenly felt uneven beneath my feet. "*Sister?*"

"Don't you know?"

I shook my head, then remembered she couldn't see me. "No."

"Well," she said hesitantly, "it's not my place, surely. I mean, this is a family privacy." She looked in my general direction. Her eyes, even though they were iced over by cataracts, were still capable of expression, and she looked like she would hold on tight to whatever she knew. I didn't want to have to say it, but we both knew there was no one left to tell me anything.

Mrs. Timberlake took a deep breath and forced the words out of her throat. "She drowned, swimming at summer camp. She was very young — maybe ten." She took her glasses off and rubbed the deep red grooves along the sides of her nose. "Things like that stick in your mind."

All the things that had been kept from me, the things that were still secrets that would never be revealed, now seemed to be suddenly boiling over. What else didn't I know? It seemed I knew nothing at all, that the bits of information that came to me were purely accidental. If I'd never asked, I wouldn't have been any the wiser. One thing was clear — death was a conspiracy. It made people get real quiet about what they knew. The way people died or left each other was too terrible to talk about, and the few things they owned or the images of themselves they inadvertently left on film were too sad to look at anymore. What I learned about my family came from people outside it. People appeared and disappeared and were never spoken of again.

I looked at the picture of my mother and Emma. Neither of them had any idea what was about to happen. My mother looked young and vulnerable in a way that

made me wish I'd been standing on the other side of her
with my arm around her shoulders. I could hear my father:
"torn asunder" was a phrase he might have used. This may
have been the last photograph of them together, taken by
someone, maybe a counselor, at the camp. They are not
posed, simply suspended for a moment in their forward
rush into summer and the lake.

And then I thought of my mother — that same Auralee
— when I knew her, and saw her standing waist deep in the
Shenandoah River, ends of hair shedding drops of water
back into its silvery coalescence — an act of complete brav-
ery. I'm sure her parents couldn't even bear to look at a
body of water, let alone wade into one. In the water, I was
her apprentice and I learned quickly and well so I could
keep up with her. She even taught me to water ski, and we
raced back and forth across the Chesapeake Bay in a rented
boat. She steered the boat, half turned around in the seat to
make sure I was still on my skis behind her, ready to circle
back to bring the tow rope within reach if I fell. In my
father's photograph of her, there she was, letting a river sur-
round her. And there she was, in my mind's eye, learning
every inch of life on the ocean floor. When she looked into
the water, did she see Emma just beneath the surface, hair
lifting like a scarf in the current? In spite of everything — in
spite of death and deep water — my mother was an excel-
lent swimmer. She had spent long summer days swimming
with me, teaching me the different strokes — breast, side,
back, butterfly — making sure I knew each one. And
though in some ways it felt as if she'd left so little to me, I

knew from all her patient teaching that of all the things that might take me unaware, it would never be water that would claim me.

After all, she had initiated me, taken me with her on one of her trips to the beach, but instead of Virginia Beach we went south, to North Carolina, all the way to Nag's Head. I had just had my first period, and she said we should do something unusual to commemorate it, that her mother had been too embarrassed to talk about it and had only shoved a box of Modess pads at her and turned away.

My mother and I made our way down the path, laden like pack mules, to Nag's Head beach. Great snarls of seaweed had washed up on the last high tide — the sea's hair yanked by the roots in the tantrum of a storm. I watched my mother make a windbreak, then a fire, amazed she knew how to do such things. I felt reassured by her movements, yet uneasy, too, at seeing her loosed from the moorings of the house.

She breathed into the fire until it took her heat and burned on its own. We cooked things wrapped in foil — corn, fish, scallions. We licked our fingers when we were done. Thin mist smeared the stars, flowed in webs up the beach. The fire burned down. Now I knew what she did when she disappeared, when she left us for those weekends, left us without a word, without a promise of her return. What was she thinking of? I never knew, never dared to ask. She was the most private person I knew, and I believed she needed me to guard that privacy because it was all she had left that was truly hers. I couldn't believe she'd let me in on it. She didn't have to say it — I could feel it, as if she whispered the actual words straight inside my ear: that if she hadn't had a family, she'd be on some remote island, or on a research vessel to the Antarctic or the inland passage of Alaska, gathering data, writing it down, making sense of the world beneath the sea.

I pulled a skinny branch from the fire and waved it in the air where the firelight couldn't quite reach, its brief after-image scribbling orange ink in the dark blue. My mother found another branch, then pretended to smoke it like a long cigarette. We laughed out loud but stuck to pantomime. I wrote crazily in the air the way I used to on the Fourth of July, with fizzing sparklers, running with fountains of sparks spewing from the white-hot center, the tiny bites nipping at my hands. I got up and ran toward the shoreline, waving the stick over my head. My mother, somewhere behind me, came running too, her longer, greener, more flexible branch sounding like a carriage whip flicking the air. We raced along the ragged line of foam, the orange tips bobbing and circling, streaking and zigzagging. I sprinted and ran far ahead, and when I looked back I could no longer see her. I thought I heard her whistle. There was still no sign of her, but there the whistle came again, shrill and clear. I ran toward her. It was so dark by then I didn't see her until it was too late to stop and we collided. We fell, tumbling in the wet sand, holding hard to each other. I started laughing. My face was pressed to hers as we rolled like kids down a grassy hill, then came to a stop. The waves caught and soaked us. We shrieked, then we laughed until we cried. It was all so unearthly and strange. I'll never forget it — the sound of our voices breaking like the waves that caught us, that fine line between the land and the ocean, between what makes sense and what is soon to be incomprehensible sorrow. Neither of us knew that she was on her way out, that unlike the tide, she wouldn't be back in again.

The Arizona sky still takes getting used to. It yawns wide over this patio, and because nothing stands in its way on any horizon, everything is visible a long way off. I can see the weather coming long before it gets here. I can see the whole wide arc of the sun's progress from east to west. Sometimes, this is soothing to me. Other times, unsettling. I can't hide here. There is no camouflage of kudzu vine, no massive, big-leafed trees. Twelve years after the fact, it's funny to think about my plans to go West, to Jack, hatched when I stood in the bus terminal parking lot in Virginia seeing a friend off. I remember trying to picture the desert where I would soon be living. I imagined it as dramatic and wild and beautiful — sand dunes sheared by wind, wild horses galloping across something called chaparral, and even wilder wolves howling at a bright yellow moon that was somehow larger and more compelling than the one that shone in my tiny attic window. Now, as I sit here on this patio, it bears no resemblance to the desert I once created in my imagination. It's a sharp place, full of things that don't want to be touched — a kind of autistic landscape that manages without any help from anyone, toughens itself continuously against needing anything, even rain.

Now Della, for one, has adapted herself — it's easy to see she belongs here. She fairly bristles with undaunted vigilance and enterprise. I suppose I never did adapt, never found the beauty here, still don't see it now. It's more exile than reward. Once, I believed that by coming here, I would be coming home. I never dreamed the journey would not have anything to do with arrival. Arizona then was a brief intermission in a life of perpetual motion. This time, I'm sitting still, and no wonder I've avoided it so long. My body may be driftless, but my mind is traveling, always traveling. Only death is completely still.

I had called the bus station in Rappahannock to see what a ticket would cost to Arizona and learned it would be sixty-five dollars and change to Phoenix, eighty dollars to Tucson. I calculated how many hours I would need to work to save it. Reverend Payne helped me find a job. It was a good job, too — or a curse; I don't know which — as a darkroom assistant at the *Mirror*, the weekly newspaper.

On my first day I walked into the plant only as far as the boss's office. But even from there I could smell the hot lead and ink and naphtha. Acrid, but for me it was the smell of freedom, of town. Every other girl I went to high school with was doing something she already knew how to do — taking in laundry, baby-sitting, waiting tables at the Blue Ridge Inn. But I was going to learn something unusual.

Callahan, that's the only name he went by and I didn't know if it was his first or last, sat me down in the one other chair in his office and looked me over with some skepticism. "What's a girl like you want with a job like this?" he asked. He took a Pall Mall out of the red pack on his desk, tamped it down and lit it. The smoke seeped into the funnel of light streaming down from his desk lamp and filled it. I felt almost guilty, as if I'd been caught in some criminal act. I tried not to, but I was squirming in that seat.

He was bald as an egg and about as round. He tipped back on his chair so that his face left the light. His voice was husky with smoke, harsh. "If I decide to give you this job you'd be working with a colored man. That bother you?" His voice crawled through the smoke.

"Why would it?" I asked. I wanted to appear nonchalant, but all of a sudden I wasn't sure. Otis, in the fourth grade, had been my only real friendship with a black person. I really didn't know what I thought about working in the dark with someone from a culture I believed in, I suppose, but had little firsthand experience with. In truth, I was nervous about the whole idea.

"Why would it bother you — you tell me. He's about seventy. Old as God." He drew on his cigarette and leaned forward suddenly. "Otherwise, missy thing, you wouldn't be goin' in the dark with him."

"Reverend Payne told me he's a master photographer."

"*Master* photographer? Grandson of a slave is probably closer to the truth." He laughed at his own joke. He pinched off the end of his half-smoked cigarette and put the rest of it back in the pack. "Good worker, I'll say that. Got his training in the army — best education in the world." He coughed, spit something into a rumpled white handkerchief he pulled out of his pants pocket. "I owe the Reverend." He looked at me, eyes narrowed. "Otherwise you wouldn't be here."

"I'm here," I said, but I don't think it had the sound of conviction.

"Well, come on then, I'll take you back there and you can get started."

We worked our way through the narrow building, past a Linotype machine, massive as the Mighty Wurlitzer I'd seen once in Radio City Music Hall in New York City. A man sat on a high seat like an ancient scribe, a keyboard in front of him. A steady stream of metal letters slid down a chute with a noise like constant, metallic rain. When he threw a lever, liquid lead seeped into the mold and the letters quickly formed into slugs with whole sentences inside them. A cylinder of lead like an anchor hung suspended over a heated cauldron, its tip submerged in the molten liquid. The man at the keyboard suddenly jumped off his seat, swore, and took a large wrench from a toolbox. He disappeared in back of the machine, shaking the wrench menacingly as he went.

From the back room I could hear the sound of the Harris press start up. The rhythm was deafening, but thrilling, like hearing a team of Clydesdales galloping down the road.

Callahan led me down a narrow flight of wooden stairs to the cellar. I must have looked more like my father than I realized, or maybe Callahan had just been saving this for last. He laughed. "Sam Grover's daughter. Thought so. I worked with him on the city desk at the *Richmond Times*

Dispatch in '42. A real *newspaperman*, not a *journalist*, as they like to call themselves today."

I nearly tripped on the bottom step. Everyone in this town knew all about me, about my family, even though we'd lived there only a little more than two years, and I was always finding out things in the oddest ways. "What did he do?"

"Drove around. He had a police radio in his car. He *lived* out there on the road, just driving until some story broke. What's he doing now? Heard he was a stringer for UP."

"He's still driving," I said. I looked at Callahan straight on, daring him to read between the lines. If he knew my father was gone, he didn't say so.

The blackest man I'd ever seen came out of a door that had a KNOCK BEFORE ENTERING sign taped to it.

"That's him, that's Jones, there," Callahan said.

His hair was almost white, his stride was slow, pain-staking, that of a man who was accustomed to standing for hours on end and had to convince his legs to stretch, to bend, in order to walk.

"Pleased to meet you," he said. He extended his hand and I couldn't help but stare — he was missing two fingers — the little and the ring.

I gripped his two-fingered hand and shook it but was afraid to hold it too firmly.

"Show her what to do," Callahan said. Then he turned to me. "If you have any trouble, you come straight to my office."

I'm sure my face turned red. I was embarrassed, not for myself, but for the stupidity of the remark on my behalf.

"I'm sorry," I wanted to say to Jones but didn't manage to move the thought to words, mostly because I was afraid he'd feel like he had to say "It doesn't matter" when it most certainly did.

He shrugged. He'd heard it all before, but his face was clamped shut, as if he had to clench his teeth to keep from saying something he truly wanted to say. "You any good at letting things ride? Got to be 'round here." He turned and headed back through the door he'd emerged from. He held it open for me. I stepped into a dark cave of a room lit by a single yellow safelight. One of its walls was rough stone, part of the foundation of the building above us. Trays of chemicals were laid out in a homemade sink, and prints hung by clothespins on a line stretched across it. The enlarger, a huge Beseler, reminded me of the kind of machine that projected stars at a planetarium. The plastic Durst I used in my darkroom in the church basement looked like a toy in comparison.

"Not much exciting happens in this town, at least not what gets printed in the paper. Here's the top story of the week — the 4-H prize winners." He held out photographs of cows, hogs, pies. "This business here — it's not meant to be some kind of hobby. And Callahan's no saint — he works you hard and yells if you mess up. And I'm sure you weren't counting on someone like me being here." He looked me directly in the eye. "You want to change your mind now, I won't hold a thing against you."

"It's not a hobby. It's not something I can stop, even if I wanted to."

"Well," he said, studying me. His face looked deep

bronze in the yellow safelight, softer now. "You'll do fine then. It takes a patient sort of person. You got to be willing to wait for it. You know how to do that — wait for things?"

I let out an exasperated sigh. I was not patient, and I knew it. I wondered how long it would take him to figure that out. But I understood waiting. Sometimes it didn't do a damn bit of good; sometimes it was all you could try to do. I didn't answer Jones's question, but the look on my face even in that muted light must have given its assent. The war I fought with patience, I was sure, would never be won. I knew — and it was a shock to admit it — that waiting was not a natural thing to me. It was something I'd resigned myself to. It was like the puppy next door, exuberant and whirling and yapping when Mr. Shipe first brought him home, but after weeks of being left alone in the yard tied to a stake, all that life leached out of him, and he lay like any dull-eyed hound on a worn patch of ground near a battered water dish. Nobody made me that way, at least not directly. I'd tamed my own restlessness by having faith in the idea of reunion.

Jones pointed to the shelf above the long sink at the neat rows of brown glass bottles, each with a meticulously hand-lettered label: D-76, Acetic Acid, Fix, Clear. He said the names out loud, and it soothed me to hear his voice intoning the familiar words in the dim, warm light. As he read off the proper mixtures from the chart he'd made on the wall, they sounded like recipes for exotic dishes. A kitchen wasn't for me — I'd flunked out of home ec because I'd cut class so much. My mother didn't like to cook. Like Jack, she didn't want anyone else in the kitchen with her when she was trying to do it. I'd always thought that sooner or later she'd get around to teaching me what she did know about it, but it never happened. At least in the darkroom, I knew where I was.

"I'll show you a trick," Jones said. He turned on the focus light for the enlarger and showed me a negative with uneven density — the head of a woman, too dark with detail. "She'd look like a ghost if I printed this straight — maybe that would be an improvement," he said, and laughed. He tucked a piece of paper on the easel, exposed the print, then dropped it into the developer tray. He rocked the print steadily as if it were some small thing in a cradle. The face materialized slowly, like someone stepping through the steam from a station-stopped train. He lifted the print from the tray and held it, dripping. "Now here's the trick. Plain old hot water." He slipped the print into another tray. In a matter of seconds, the woman's features began to fill in where before there had been only vagueness, like indistinct markings in snow, before.

In two weeks' time Jones had taught me enough to keep up with the demands of the *Mirror*. But Callahan didn't trust me with his film. I heard him pull into the back parking lot — there was a hole in the muffler of his ancient Hudson, and the dry hinges shrieked when the lid opened on the trunk where he kept his equipment. He came in the back door dressed in white like an ice cream vendor, but with a white straw hat. Inside the hat were the telltale signs of black hair dye melted in the heat — visible on the hatband when he took it off and held it in his hand.

"Are you sure you know what to do?" he asked, unwilling to hand over his day's work. "Jones — he takes them and works some kind of magic or voodoo or I don't know what all, but they come out, those pictures, they come out every single time. Now don't you mess 'em up."

"I won't," I said. Despite Callahan's comical appearance, Jones had told me he wielded authority like a small hammer, and that if I was smart and quick I could avoid getting knocked in the head with it.

"Well I surely hope you mean it because there's some things I can't go back and reshoot. The show's over, the people have gone on home." He thrust his hands in his coat pockets, which looked stretched from the repetition of that gesture. He fiddled with coins and keys and probably a few spare flashbulbs before he produced the film.

I took it from him. The paper that wrapped around the end of the rolls felt sticky with his perspiration, and I could hardly bear to touch it. But I developed it quickly, accurately. I wasn't worried. Jones had told me to underdevelop all of Callahan's film because he always overexposed it. Some people, it seemed, were entirely predictable, and once you learned their quirks and habits you could compensate for them, especially with chemistry. Maybe only with chemistry.

I thrived on what Jones taught me. I ate it up. It seemed he knew a thousand things about photography that weren't written in books. Tried and true like folk medicine. He could fix mistakes of light, balancing the too much and too little with dodging and burning, an elaborate, graceful dance done slowly with the hands. It seemed there was no negative he couldn't get a picture out of. "It's in there, waiting to get let out," he'd say. "It's just a matter of getting it to come to you."

Jones had lost his wife, Ada, in a car accident the same time he lost his fingers. He had a picture of her in the darkroom. "She keeps her eye on me." The woman who kept her eye on him was caught by the camera, seemingly suspended in midair — a young woman in a white dress leaping over a driftwood log, arms flung wide for balance, a braid flying beneath a hat, the surf behind her as white as the slip that showed a little below her hem.

Next to Ada's picture a luminous woman stood with her head bowed inside a red frame. If you looked at it from the right side you could see her. If you moved to the left she shimmered and melted and gave way to a manifestation of a crucified Jesus. They had the same long hair. "She's the Virgin of Guadalupe. Thomas, my cousin, brought her up from Mexico City." There was also a votive candle, a small statue of a golden-haired white girl, a scorpion in amber, a postcard from St. Louis, a silver dollar with a hole shot clean through it, a cherry bomb, a pair of wire-rimmed glasses with both lenses gone.

"Souvenirs and charms," he said. With the light on, all these things were distinct. With the safelight on, they took on an amber glow and seemed to run together, creating an irregular connected skyline like a city or a mountain range. And there was Ada's wild leap over both of us now. I wondered what she would think of me.

"The army showed me more of the world than I want-

ed to see. Some things I never will get out of my mind —
people getting killed, children hungry and their homes
gone. Families with no fathers."

My own father hadn't gone to the war; he'd only report-
ed on it. He'd written scores of articles but never kept the
newspapers they were printed in.

I sent Jack a letter to tell him about my job, about how I
was saving for a ticket to come to see him. The fact that he
hadn't written to me first didn't give me pause, though it
should have. I assumed that being family gave me a standing invitation.

Despite the distractions of the job, I couldn't stop waiting for a letter back. At first I blamed the delay on the post
office. There'd been a scandal in the paper about postal
employees drinking on the job and a photograph by Callahan of several empty bottles of Old Grandad wedged
between a heap of mail sacks. Jack's letters could have fallen
down a heating grate or been forgotten in some pile on a
loading dock in Tucson for all I knew. I even began to sus-
pect that Mrs. Timberlake was destroying my mail; nearly
blind, though, she probably wouldn't risk it since she might
accidentally get rid of some of her own.

Another week went by and nothing came. I woke up at
exactly 3:58 every morning, shocked to find out how far I
was from dawn, how horrifyingly exact my internal clock
had become, how ready my mind was at that hour, sharpening itself on the bleak edge of dread. I drank a lot of
coffee, which I made on a hot plate in my room, and felt so
attuned to every nuance of light and sound in the world I

became exhausted from noticing it all. I memorized the intricate calls of birds, I heard the ring coming to the phone before the signal actually came down the wire. I had a second hand inside my head and no longer required a timer in the darkroom. I saw things in the developing image before they were actually there. I felt radioactive. Luminous. Even dangerous. I could feel the relentless flow of blood in my veins. I felt and heard everything, but I couldn't feel my father or my mother. I almost couldn't feel Jack anymore. I'd lost the signals of my family. All that was left was a kind of wild ringing in my ears.

I wished I had something to put alongside of Jones's things on the shelf, something with power in it, a power that had pull in the world. I had nothing except a picture of Jack. I propped it on the shelf next to the Virgin of Guadalupe because she had influence in his part of the country. Jones looked at it suspiciously but didn't ask who it was or why I'd put it there.

The following week there was a postcard with a picture of a coyote howling at the desert sky. Jack only wrote a few lines, congratulating me on getting the job, hoping I was not working too hard — the kind of neutral words people wrote in yearbooks. He said he'd started his own business, making furniture, that he was tired of working for people who didn't care about quality. "Wish me luck," he said. He signed it, simply, "Jack." Not "Love," not "Yours truly," not even "Sincerely." Just Jack. The disappointment at not receiving the heart-to-heart letter I'd wanted was crushing, but I sat right down and wrote him back, filled six pages with details about the *Mirror*, about Jones, about all the things I was learning. I mailed it that afternoon. Then I began waiting all over again.

I made mistakes at work. I ruined a roll of Callahan's film by pouring in the hypo-clear before the developer and had to hear about it from him for a week afterward. Every time he'd hand me a new roll to develop, a dark look on his heat-red face and the admonition "Guard that with your life."

"You got trouble at home?" Jones asked as he measured chemicals and poured them through the funnel.

"I don't know what you mean," I said, stirring the Dektol viciously in the warm water, furious that it took so long to dissolve.

"Then why bring that picture in here — or don't you know yourself?"

"It's my brother!" I said, as calmly as I could, but my voice was horrible and loud in that small space where a whisper would have sufficed. "I got a letter from him the other day."

"So, what's the problem?"

"It's not a problem. It's simple. I just have to talk to him."

"Brother and sister much simpler than that."

I flailed at the black curtain to get out of there, to go to the ladies' room, which was always private since I was the only female in the place. I felt dizzy, sick to my stomach. I headed straight for the sink and leaned over it to splash some cold water on my face. I raised my head and saw my face in the mirror, dripping. I leaned toward myself, hands braced against the cool porcelain. It was certainly not the first time I'd seen myself in a mirror. I could hardly believe my eyes. Jones was right. I'd made everything complicated. All I knew was I felt hungry, like I was walking around thin, and worse than that, that I couldn't think of what I was really hungry for. I was afraid I was fading, that I had limited time to have an effect, to be remembered.

I'd been living on wild hope, and suddenly it seemed a bridge to nowhere, a rope bridge fraying so fast there was no way back and no way forward. So I threw myself into my work, hoping it would catch me. Not just the work at the paper printing Callahan's news pictures, but taking my own, the kind of images that didn't make the news: patterns of light on water, abandoned houses leaning away from their foundations, rusted rivets on a steel bridge — just things that wanted my attention, wanted to be taken like money on the ground.

Less of me thought about Jack and more of me looked to what I was doing. Light at least was something I could calculate. I began to get a sixth sense about correct exposures, learned how to read negatives. Instead of reversed representations of the real world that I had to swap in my head — the dark areas really light, the light dark — I began to see them as a whole, a process. I imagined it was not unlike the point in learning a foreign language where you begin to dream in it. I would get a strong hunch what the correct exposure would be, and the moment when the image cohered in the developer tray at the right interval confirmed my guess. I couldn't trust my heart very well, but slowly I began to believe in my imagination.

When I was tired, when I could no longer see straight to focus the camera, I'd walk to my favorite, secluded place on the Rappahannock River, a deep pool beneath an overhanging willow tree. I'd shed my clothes behind a bush and wade in, watch the water make its way around me — little eddies swirled around my calves. One afternoon I had an eerie feeling I wasn't alone, that my secret swimming place had been discovered. I looked around but didn't see anyone. I waded in, let the water rise to my collarbone. I could hear the distant clatter of a car crossing the wooden bridge downstream. Treading water in the green gold-shot light, I imagined if I let go, I could drift like Ophelia. Would it take hours or days to go a hundred miles? I would drift right by the cabin we rented on the Shenandoah when my mother was still alive, and there she'd still be, standing waist deep, and might or might not grab me as I floated by. I would drift past the place where her sister Emma went down. I would come out at last at the ocean where my mother and I built a fire. I could keep going forever. I looked at my body in the green water. My breasts were swollen. A thin thread of blood unraveled from between my legs and was carried slowly downstream.

I heard a sound in the woods. Sticks snapped, leaves crackled like fire. I saw a face in the leaves, the flash of light on glasses. Dark hair. The musical prodigy. Ben.

He stepped forward. There were long scratches across his knees from the thicket of blackberry bushes behind him. He stood on the bank looking skinny and sun-struck and more exposed than I was — at least I had the veil of water around me — only my head and shoulders were for certain. I stirred the water with my hands. Whatever he could see was distorted by sunlight strained through water. My body was no longer a solid, but liquid, a shifting shape inside a river.

"Did you follow me?"

"This isn't the first time."

"So why aren't you hiding this time?" I felt indignant — it didn't occur to me to be scared — that he'd been in the bushes watching me strip and swim.

"How many times?"

"A few."

"What do you want?"

"I don't know." Now he looked defensive, as if he were the one naked in the water and had just been found out.

"Are you coming in or are you just going to spy on me?"

"I'm not spying." He pulled his striped T-shirt over his head, exposing a mushroom-white chest. His nipples looked like tiny brown welts, bee-stings. He pulled off his shoes and socks, then removed his glasses and wristwatch and placed them carefully inside his left shoe. He pulled his shorts down but left his boxers on and waded right in. The thin cotton fabric ballooned in the current.

He was a contradiction — so fragile he looked as if even the wind could push him around, yet persistent as a fish moving against a strong current.

"You're so white," I said, looking at his chest.

"I'm not supposed to be in the sun. I burn easy." His arms spread wide like long wings, revealing small tufts of dark hair. "Sometimes I wish I were black, don't you?"

"What for?"

"They move like they actually live inside their bodies." He folded his arms in again. "In church last week the sermon was about Adam and Eve, about the danger of wanting something you can't have. What I think is that when they were thrown out of Eden they were really sent away — from their own bodies." He flung his right arm out, pointed his finger somewhere beyond the trees. "Excommunicated. Flunked out of Paradise. What I think Eden was really about was the pleasure of being human." He dropped his arm and it broke the water with only a small splash. "Most of the time my body feels like something straining against a leash."

I looked at him. He looked back. His eyes were a deep hazel green, like the color of the river. The way he spoke startled me — it was the same way my father talked — that grand sweep above common conversation.

"I have epilepsy," he said.

That one short sentence brought me back to earth. I bent my knees until the water rose to my chin. "Does it scare you?"

"I never know when it's going to happen — it could happen two minutes from now." He smacked the water with his hand, sending up a spray. "There isn't time to be scared. It's like lightning — you don't feel it when it hits you, and you don't figure it out until you find yourself on the ground."

I had never known anyone with epilepsy, wondered if he would feel somehow different, a certain dark volatility beneath the pale calm. I sank down another inch until the water touched my lips.

"Why are you hiding? You don't need to — I've already seen that picture of you."

"This is different."

I closed my eyes. I felt the sun on my face at the same moment my body called up its private terror, always waiting in the wings. The memory in the muscles — my body submerged, then rising from a bath because a stranger told me to. I told myself I was not there, not two years ago, not in New Jersey at the mercy of a man who'd only given me a ride and then wanted everything I had in return. I was here, in Virginia, with Ben, in the river. I could turn away if I wanted to.

I stayed where I was. I opened my eyes. I watched Ben wade slowly toward me, naked and vulnerable — to the sun that could burn him, to the lightning that could strike his mind at any moment. I touched him on the shoulder. His skin was warm. He lifted my arms and put them around his waist. The river made its way around the new shape we made. I rested my chin on his shoulder. The ends of his hair were wet. My hands slid down over his sharp shoulder blades and rested on the small of his back. His hands lifted me under my arms and my legs rose until they wrapped around his waist. On dry land we would be awkward, but the river made us weightless. We stayed just like that a long time without moving. I could hear the muffled zing of dragonflies, the rasp of a crow, the leathery sound of leaves stropping each other in the breeze. I smelled my hair, fragrant as grass, part wet, part dry from the hat of sunlight upon my head. And I felt Ben, real as anything around me.

I don't remember unwrapping myself from him, striding slowly back to the bank, shy again once out of water.

We walked back to town. Our hands, separate, kept brushing against one another. Finally, we just held them. We didn't talk. The air thickened with humid dusk, and the sounds of frogs and insects started up as if the darkness were a lonely void that had to be filled with sound until dawn came to take it back. A shape came toward us, moving no faster than we were. As we got closer, the shape materialized into the stooped posture of a tired woman going home, probably after polishing a dining room table she would never be allowed to sit down at. She was about to cross the boundary between two worlds, one where water ran in pipes and the bathroom was a room inside the house, to the world where water was still carried in buckets and jars from a pump out back.

"Evening," she said softly as she passed us, and it seemed less a greeting than an announcement that the day was over, the light definitively gone, a last warning before the full force of night came down.

When we reached Mrs. Timberlake's house we stood outside on the sidewalk. I held him again, felt the blades of his shoulders, softened just a little beneath the cotton shirt, and I thought about his version of Adam and Eve. I traced the arc of bone and felt it as the place on the body where wings were once attached. Aeons ago it must have been jagged, but over time it had been sanded down as the memory of flight faded and the body forgot and began to look at birds with an inexplicable longing, even a kindredness it couldn't explain.

That day part of me drifted toward him like a water strider toward a small island, a part I would never be able to reel back in again. I felt an aching sadness along with my first desire. "Oh, Matty," he'd said in a whisper, his breath grazing my neck like a wish.

I squeezed Ben's hand at the driveway. He hesitated for half a second, then headed for home. I stood there watching his white shorts scissoring away in the dark. I turned toward Mrs. Timberlake's house. Some child's tortured scales poured out the window, then Mrs. Timberlake's strident assessments followed. I heard the scrape of the piano stool, the shuffle of sheet music, the irregular rhythm their shoes made together as they entered the foyer. Silhouettes pushed the screen door open and stepped outward into the evening: Mrs. Timberlake filling the frame, throwing a lean shadow across the porch that rippled down the stairs; a young girl loping down the porch steps hit the sidewalk at a dead run. She didn't even see me. She was night-blind and I was a shadow outside the lightfall of the house. She picked up speed as she raced past me, disappeared like some wild thing running for her life down the darkened road.

News from Mississippi reached Rappahannock slowly. The South, as a region, was starting to shed an old, old skin, but small towns clung to the old disguise. The *Mirror* ran a two-column-inch story on page six about lunch counter sit-ins, children blasted with firehoses in plain sight. What made the front page that week in our town was the Gold Cup races — an elaborate steeplechase that transported the wealthy to the England they all felt entitled to. Callahan got it all — the Rolls Royces gleaming in the meadow, the nervous horses nearby, the uniformed butlers serving their employers who sat on blankets amid candelabra, crystal and silver, and folded linen. Far below, the thoroughbreds vaulted across an elaborate maze of hedges and ditches. The people on the hill watched it all through opera glasses held in one hand while they sipped from crystal champagne goblets in the other. Carolyn was probably among them now with her blue-blood fiancé.

Meanwhile, on the other side of town, the black people gathered. Nothing looked much different on Main Street, but I could feel something change even as I walked down the sidewalk. The blank, hot, afternoon gazes were sharpening into outright stares at those who walked past them. The old men sat, as they always did, on a tier of the post office steps, exchanging news, greeting passersby. By the end of the week, a NO LOITERING sign appeared on the steps — an odd instruction that didn't seem to apply to them. They ignored the signs. They weren't loitering. They seemed to be waiting now. Waiting for something to happen.

Carolyn had made me promise to meet her for lunch. As I came down Main Street from the *Mirror* I saw the postmaster lean out the front door, half of him still sheltered inside. He peered outside nervously, bald and pink in the noonday sun.

"You people got to move on now — these steps were never intended to be sat on all day long."

No one moved. In fact, no one even looked at him. I stopped, glad I had my camera. It was my one constant accessory now — I carried it instead of a purse. I took a picture from across the street. The men on the steps faced straight toward me as if I'd asked them to pose for a class picture, the taller ones in the back. Ruining the symmetry, dead center, was the white man, his mouth wide open, his arm pointing away in a direction nobody wanted to go.

The sheriff pulled up in a patrol car just then with the single red light twirling on top, but no siren. He maneuvered into the no-parking zone in front. He climbed slowly out of the patrol car and left the light on for effect, but the effect dissipated in the noon glare. He stood, hands on skinny hips, surveying the group from under the wide brim of his hat.

"You folks move along now — you're breaking the law, as you can see by the sign there. I'm going on down to the courthouse. I'll be there about ten minutes. When I come back, I expect you to be gone."

He didn't wait for a response, just swung himself back into the car and headed slowly down the street, looking in the rearview mirror the whole way. I expected something to happen, but the men had obviously already agreed among themselves beforehand and had no need to discuss it further. They continued to sit, as if step-sitting were a God-given right of any person, particularly a Southerner. It was unthinkable that they would be deprived of it.

I went to the drugstore, checked the lunch counter, but didn't see Carolyn. I waited a few minutes then rushed back to the post office. By the time I got back the steps were jammed with at least fifty people.

True to his word, the sheriff came back in exactly ten minutes, with several deputies. One of them had a police dog — a German shepherd on a leash — that I'd never seen before, and I wondered if police departments all over the South had just been issued one for such occasions. The dog looked bored and just sat on the sidewalk. No one moved. The police radio crackled inside the car. And then a Coke bottle sailed out from somewhere on the tier of steps and hit the sidewalk, its thick green glass breaking into large, jagged chunks. Everyone stared at it as if it might miraculously reassemble itself. The sheriff whirled around to the deputy with the German shepherd and gave him a signal. The deputy said something to the dog, and the chain grew taut as it strained forward, set into motion like something mechanical in which a key had just been turned. The dog started barking frantically. The men on the steps stood up slowly, almost majestically, like a choir getting ready to sing. The sheriff stepped forward. I focused fast, watched it all happen through the viewfinder. I moved in closer. Then everything broke apart. People scattered when two more policemen surged out of the post office door.

The chaos of people, running and flailing, together with the rhythmic lunging of the dog, were all barely contained in that two-and-a-quarter-inch frame. If I'd seen it head-on I would have been scared, but I looked through the viewfinder as if it were a periscope in treacherous waters. I was invisible. At least for the moment, until I heard Carolyn call my name.

I turned around. Carolyn was just coming across the street toward me but stopped as soon as she stepped off the curb. She looked surprised, then confused.

A hand grabbed my shoulder. "Just what in hell do you think you're doing here?" the sheriff said.

I turned and took his picture — a yelling mouth, eyes

hidden behind sunglasses. "I work for the paper," I said, then wished I hadn't.

"Get out of here before you get hurt or arrested or both," he yelled. I moved away but only halfway back across the street. He watched me but then got distracted.

Carolyn came up behind me. "Are you crazy?" she said, her voice high-pitched and frightened. Then her voice shifted — I wasn't looking at her because I was afraid to take my eyes off the people on the steps. She started yelling at me in the middle of the street. "Get over here where you belong!"

I whirled around and stared at her. For a second I saw an ancient hatred come into her face — the hatred handed down by families that keeps the boundary lines so firmly drawn.

The dog, now off his leash, lunged toward a man on the steps and knocked him backward, then went for him as he struggled to right himself again. I ran to get close. A rose of blood began to bloom on the white sleeve of the man's shirt. I leaned in. I raised my head from the viewfinder that had already shown me his face. *Jones.* The dog was still hanging on. My finger stayed on the shutter, but I couldn't press the lever down.

"Take it!" he said through clenched teeth.

My finger moved. The shutter opened, then closed.

"Now run!"

I walked quickly across the street and saw Carolyn's face, shocked but safe, pressed up against the display window inside the furniture store where she must have fled when hell broke loose. Superimposed over her frozen features were the reflections of people scattering, running. I couldn't stop myself. I raised the camera, took that image with me —

the face of someone who once knew all my secrets, gladly given, who now looked at me as if I were someone she no longer recognized. Then I ran, clutching the camera.

A squad car followed me down the street. I ran up the alley. I flew through the back door of the *Mirror* and literally dove into the darkroom, locking the door behind me. I cranked the film back into the cassette and pulled it out of the camera. My hands were shaking so badly I could hardly wind the film onto the reel. I slammed it into the can and poured the developer in, then had to make myself slow down as I agitated it. Gradually, the rhythm of it, the five-seconds-motion every minute took over. My breathing slowed, and by the time I poured the developer out my hands were nearly steady again. I finished the processing and hung the film to dry. I stepped out of the darkroom and headed for the water cooler in the front office. A policeman stood at the counter. I stopped dead in my tracks, then backed up. He didn't see me. He was leaning over the counter, speaking intently to Callahan. I went quickly back to the darkroom, took the film down, and hung it in the closet behind a stack of cartons. I loaded a new roll of film into the Rollei and advanced it to the last frame. There was a knock on the door, and Callahan's voice calling me. He stood there with the sheriff. "I'll take that film." I looked at Callahan. He shrugged and nodded. "Give it to him," he said.

I brought the camera out. I rewound the film slowly. I gave the sheriff the blank cassette. He pulled the leader out and exposed the film, then handed it back to me. "We don't need anybody any more stirred up out there than they already are. Now you just keep out of it." He strode down

the hall in his heavy boots, leaving Callahan and me standing there.

"He can't do that," I said.

"He can. His brother owns the paper." I couldn't tell
from looking at him what he felt about it. "I've got to bail
Jones out. I want you to get those Gold Cup pictures done
by the time I get back — we've got a deadline this afternoon, or have you forgotten that?"

I made myself go back to work. I printed the photos of
the races and left them on Callahan's desk. He hadn't come
back by the time I left.

I took my film home with me and went to work. I made
a print of the last shot — Jones's face coming clear, the dog
attached to his arm. I couldn't believe it was him. And the
picture of Carolyn — a ghost, a bride-to-be behind glass,
partly erased by the random pattern of people running for
their lives.

I called Jones at home. A woman answered. "Who's
this?" she demanded when I asked for him.

"Matty, from the paper — a friend."

She put the phone down and it clunked on some hard
surface. I heard light steps going away and heavier steps
coming back.

"Hello?" I recognized Jones's voice. It seemed odd to be
talking to him on the telephone.

"Did you print it?"

"The sheriff almost got it. But it's safe — it's home with
me."

"Listen, you send that picture to the *Washington Post*. I
know a man working there."

Jones gave me the name and address of his friend —
Tom Dunne at the Sunday magazine. Before I hung up, I
asked him about his arm. "I still have it" was all he said, but
the bitterness in his voice frightened me. I told him I'd see
him soon, though I had no idea how long that would be,
since he said that Callahan had told him to take a few days
off, to wait for things to cool down.

Jones's arm healed, but inwardly I festered. While the
girl I used to ride bikes and sneak beers with was planning
her wedding, I was sending off a photograph to the *Washington Post* of a black man with a white man's dog tearing at
his arm.

It didn't take long for the *Post* to respond. I stood on the
other side of the front desk while I took the call.

Callahan watched me carefully as he marked contact
sheets.

"We'd like to run your photo — we already got a release
from the man in the picture."

"When?" I stole a glance at Callahan. He was staring
right at me. I was sure he could somehow hear the other
side of the conversation.

"We run the picture next Sunday in the magazine, and I
send you a hundred dollars. For one Sunday people will
look at it. A few might not be able to forget it."

I hung up the phone.

"No personal calls — no boyfriends on company time,"
Callahan declared.

"It wasn't personal," I said, which was the truth. The
photograph was about to become public. Its publication, I
knew, would be like a match thrown on gas-soaked tinder. I

marched past him and had half a mind to turn around, set him straight. It was all I could do to bite my tongue.

The *Post* sent me a copy of the Sunday magazine in advance of the day the paper was to come out. The photograph of Jones was one of four printed under the heading FREEDOM — ARE WE ONLY HALFWAY THERE? It seemed a good question, given the images beneath it. My picture was the largest and most frightening. The German shepherd lunged from the lower left toward the center, which was Jones, holding out his arm to protect himself, and the dog's teeth made contact; together they made a strange hybrid. A policeman stood by, hands on hips, face invisible, watching. Beneath the photo, an italic caption: *Racial tension in Rappahannock, Virginia.* Sideways, alongside the photo, tiny letters in all caps formed my name: PHOTO BY MEREDITH GROVER. Inside, along with the article, was the picture of Carolyn looking grim and scared. I'd sent it along as an afterthought; I'd forged her signature on the release form. It was too good a picture not to use.

Sunday arrived and the *Post* didn't, at least not on time. I was disappointed, maybe a little relieved. I fully expected to be run out of town when the paper hit the street. Meanwhile, Rappahannock was celebrating the Fourth of July the same way it celebrated anything else — the Epworth League set up folding tables on the church lawn, the men gravitated to the horseshoe pitch as if it were an irresistible magnet that pulled them from the outfield of their lives toward a common center. Someone had organized a tug-of-war and sack races for the kids, and Johnny Ace and the

Rebel Yells, a bluegrass band from Amisville, took the better part of an hour to test out the microphones that Reverend Payne had set up by stringing together a multi-colored snake of every extension cord in town to an outlet in the church vestibule. Halfway through the first song they blew a fuse. They finally gave up on amplification and just sang loud, winning the instant admiration of everyone for getting through a trying time in public. Nobody danced, exactly, but feet moved anyhow, as if they couldn't help themselves. A two-year-old toddled up to Johnny Ace and stared, mouth open for a while, then squealed and began to chug up and down to the music.

I had set up a little booth to take portraits for a dollar each. Half would go to the church — my way of paying rent for darkroom space — and half to my fund for my great escape, which might have to happen sooner now than I had planned. I hung a black drape I'd found in the church basement and set a chair in front of it. I took pictures while the light lasted. I must have photographed everyone in town that afternoon. I was just about to shut it down when Carolyn came and sat in the chair.

She leaned forward, hands squarely on her knees. "My father says we can sue you." She sat back, rested her hands on the arms of the chair. "But I told him it wasn't worth the bother." She crossed her legs and her foot bobbed nervously in its black, T-strap shoe. She seemed to be trying hard to contain herself, but maybe it was my silence that finally provoked her. The words came flying out as if she'd stayed up all night rehearsing them.

"What happened to you? I used to really like you — I

used to want to *be* you in the seventh grade. When you ran
away, I was still your friend even when everyone said to stay
away from you, when they wouldn't even let you back in
school or the goddamn Girl Scouts. I stuck by you. I *waited*
for you. Then you go and shit on me like this. You don't
know when to stop. You never did."

"I never asked you to wait," I said, the blood pounding
behind my eyes, the back of my neck suddenly hot and cold
with sweat.

Carolyn stood up, slung her purse strap so hard over her
shoulder her purse swung open, and at least half of what
was in it fell out. I got down on my hands and knees to
retrieve her keys, glad to have something to do besides take
her accusations. She grabbed the keys from my hand, swept
the lipstick and compact and Kotex into the mouth of her
purse. "*Selfish!*" she cried. "I was going to ask you to take the
pictures of my wedding — well, you can forget it. You've
taken the last picture of me you'll ever get."

Carolyn left me there on the ground. I began to wish I
were in the picture instead of her, so it would be my face,
the way it felt now — serious and scared, looking through
thin glass at the world.

"Nigger lover," a man called out to me as he walked past
my booth, but I couldn't see his face. Once again the town
had had enough of me. When I ran away that time, people
literally shunned me on the streets, at the A&P. And now
I'd just pushed my last friend away. But then it hit me —
I was now part of a cause I'd only stumbled onto. I really
didn't know what I was doing — it's not as if I'd done it with
conscious conviction. More than anything, I was mad at

Rappahannock. Maybe, as Carolyn said, I *was* selfish, had used this opportunity to take my own private revenge. I cared about Jones because I knew him, but now Jones stood for something bigger, something gaining momentum. I'd set something in motion without exactly meaning to, and it scared the hell out of me.

I saw Ben standing in line at the barbecue table. It seemed to me he was the only person left in the world who would still talk to me. I pushed my way through people who whispered, passing the Sunday magazine around. I grabbed Ben's hand and pulled him out of there as if I were being pursued. We ran all the way to the river.

"Stop!" he gasped, trying to catch his breath.

I doubled over, pushing the palms of my hands against my thighs for balance, my hair nearly brushing the grass.

"They hate me, don't they? I've made their shitty little town look bad."

"You didn't *make* it look bad — you only showed what was already there."

"That's not the way they see it."

I straightened up. My hair spilled back to my shoulders, exposing my frightened face. Ben reached toward me.

I let my hands do what they had wanted to ever since that day in the water. I unbuttoned his shirt, then pushed it off his shoulders. This was not the romantic moment that I'd long dreamed I would come to, but a desperate act, as if my days were numbered and I had to push myself hard toward something I'd always imagined should be gentle.

Sunlight flashed through the leaves — light pulsed over everything, like a code I couldn't read. Ben changed in front of my eyes into a person inside a trance, eyes open, his mind working inside another world.

"Hey," I said, but he didn't seem to hear me.

His eyes rolled back as if he were looking straight inside his skull. Then he pitched forward onto the grass. He started convulsing, as if some animal had him in its teeth or the earth itself shook him like a fly from its massive flank. I knelt down beside him, my hand reaching helplessly toward him, afraid to touch.

And then it stopped as suddenly as it started. Ben came back from wherever he'd been — caught out in the storm inside his brain. Light no longer flashed through the leaves; it had gone inside of him. The sun was a flat disk behind a cloud. I lay down next to him, and our breathing slowed until we breathed deeply, in tandem like a single four-legged thing.

I knew his touch was coming, but I did not know that in the moment he came inside me, when I gave the things, finally, that women give, that I would feel mostly like a furious girl. I fought for breath as if I'd been running a long, long way. I fought the urge to cry out loud. We were reaching back through the open gates of Eden, but for all our human pleasure, our lips were sealed, as if sound alone could give us away.

Jones and I left the *Mirror* for good on the same day. I was "let go," as Callahan put it. He wouldn't let me out of his sight as I gathered up my things. Jones came into the darkroom — his first day since the dog tore his arm. It was still in a sling. Right to Callahan's face he said, loud and clear, "I've been with you a long time — long enough. Anyone looks for me here, you tell them as of today I don't work for you anymore."

Callahan's face loomed in the red-orange light — a round, frowning moon. "My hands are tied on this one — it's the sheriff leaning on his brother." He held out his hands to his sides, palms up, as if there was no help for it. "I'm sure as hell not willing to get my ass fired over *this*," Callahan said. He yanked the chain on the overhead light. At any other time it would have been a sacrilege. Now it didn't matter. Still, it was unnatural — all that glaring light in a place that had been such a sanctuary. He pushed past us through the black-curtained door. Jones turned the light off again.

He took the picture of Ada down from the shelf. He put the picture inside the box, then the candle, then the silver dollar, the scorpion, the Virgin of Guadalupe, the cherry bomb. I watched him take these things down one at a time, slowly, and to each object he gave his full attention. His composure was more frightening than his anger.

"What are you going to do?"

Jones closed the flaps on the cardboard box. His hands were trembling, and I knew it wasn't age — he was steady as a surgeon. It was anger rising again from deep in the bones.

"My son Raymond, from Washington, gets here tomorrow on a chartered bus — they're going to hook up with the Freedom Riders in Birmingham." He looked at me, slightly calmer now. "I'm going with him."

He reached inside the box and handed me the Virgin of Guadalupe. "Take this," he said. "I've got Ada. You need someone to watch out for you."

I looked at his face. His skin shone like dark brass in the yellow light. His eyes liquid and deep and patient and, I realized now, very, very old.

I wanted to put my arms around him but I didn't know how to begin. It was too late, or too soon, for a lot of things. The town would change after both of us left it. In a few years the senior prom would have both black and white couples dancing; another decade and there would be mixed couples. But right then we were so far away from that, from each other. Jones and I may have worked together, even been friends, but affection was held in, like playing a close hand, wary, but safer.

I got a ride to the station with the postman so I could see Jones leave for Alabama. An old school bus that said CHAR-TER on the front idled in the parking lot. The people already inside the bus coming from Washington had opened the windows wide and were singing. Then I saw Jones standing inside a small circle of relations wishing him off.

I'd never seen him look so happy. It was hard to be sad. I gave him a sealed envelope with the hundred dollars I'd gotten for the photo. I knew he wouldn't take it if he knew what it was. He put it in the box he had tucked beneath his arm. He thanked me. As I turned away, I saw the sheriff's car parked on the edge of the lot, he and his deputy leaning casually up against it, their eyes hidden beneath their hats and dark glasses.

The driver honked the horn and Jones got on. The door swung closed, sealed with a brief suck of air. The bus started rolling. Hands waved out the windows. Hands in the parking lot waved back. The bus lurched through the potholes like a great ark dipping into the swells. Then it climbed the slight rise onto the highway and gained speed, shifting upward through the gears. I envied them, going off toward a freedom they believed in, as if freedom were a new country one could rightfully drive toward, arrive in, and be welcomed into. I'd played only a bit part, and now it was over.

When the bus was out of sight, I felt despair settle over me, invisible and deadly as nerve gas. The idea of staying in Virginia any longer was unbearable. Jones's leaving was throwing out a tow line. I was going to reach out and grab it, not to follow him, but to use his momentum to get myself out of there. I wasn't just going to sit in Rappahannock and wait any longer. Why wait until I turned eighteen — what was the point?

I walked into the station and went over to the ticket counter. I slid my sixty-five dollars across the counter. "I want a one-way ticket to Tucson," I said.

The clerk squinted at me.

"That's in Arizona," I told him.

He thumbed through his book, ran his stubby finger down the rows of destinations. "Long way," he said.

"Tomorrow," I said.

He raised his eyebrows but didn't comment, though he looked as if he wanted to. He took my money and wrote it up. "Change in Atlanta, then change in Dallas, then again in

Phoenix. Takes three days, but they stop for food." He handed me the ticket in a little envelope. It seemed too small and thin to give me passage anywhere.

There was a map under the glass of the counter. I traced my finger across the country, across the Mississippi, across the breadth of prairie to Arizona — a landlocked state whose shape was so much simpler and squarer than those in the East. The town of Oracle where Jack lived was not even on the map. For the first time since I'd decided to go, I felt uncertain. I had an image of the Greyhound sailing off the rim of the Grand Canyon in the dark, falling into that natural wonder with no more sound than a stone.

When you know for certain you're going to leave a place, everything in it feels crowded, as if the place itself can't wait for you to go. The light that formerly settled benevolently over the town began to ravage it. Trees blocked my view. The kudzu strangled the woods, would not rest until it had devoured everything, even the telephone poles. The humidity was a force that pushed down on me, squeezing the sweat from my skin. I'd never wanted to come to Virginia in the first place. As far as I was concerned, I wasn't leaving a minute too soon.

I hadn't counted on how shocked Ben would be when I told him I was going, but then I hadn't given it much thought. We were sitting on the stone steps of his front porch. His parents were watching television — I could hear their laughter from deep inside the house.

I told him that I wasn't coming back, that I had to go to my brother. As soon as I said that, I knew how awful it sounded. It was as if I were breaking up with Ben so I could run off with Jack, that I'd only used him until I could have what I really wanted.

"Just like that." He said it like a statement, not a question.

I couldn't look at him. I wanted to bolt. I wanted him to understand. But I didn't quite understand it myself. It was something I was driven to do, not a thing I'd calmly thought out. Whatever thinking I'd done had taken place alone in my attic room.

"Come with me. To the station," I said.

"Isn't it a little late?" He stood up, his hand already on the screen door to go inside. "You don't need anybody to see you off. It'll just slow you down."

"Don't go. I just don't know how to say this right."

"Well, what *do* you know, Matty? Not yourself. You don't know yourself very well at all. You want to know what I think? You're just like your father." His voice changed. It was almost pleading. "Why don't you stay? Is it so awful here? Is it really so hard to stick around?"

I reached for his hand.

"Don't," he said. "Just leave it alone, Matty. Do what you need to do. Just go." His hand tightened on the door. "Shit," he said.

He pushed the door open and slammed it behind him. The latch clicked and held.

I sat there, stunned. I couldn't make my feet move. A new feeling flooded every vein. Heartsick. That's what I'd call it. That's what I felt when he walked into the house — the house where I used to live.

Ben's light went on in my old room. He leaned out over the sill, and I saw in his shape something of myself reaching for my father's headlights as he backed out the driveway. I stood beneath the window and looked up. Something fluttered from the sill. Scraps of paper fell like a brief snow. It was my picture — the one I had taken of myself, naked, that I'd left on the closet door. Fragments of myself littered the lawn. An open eye, a closed mouth, a leg, part of a breast. My hands shook as I gathered them up. He disappeared from the window, then came back a few seconds later with something cupped in his hands, then threw that, too, into the air. A flash of white wings, a streamer of a tail. He'd never told me that he had a bird. One more well-kept secret. I didn't even know what kind of bird it was. I thought it might plummet to the ground, that it had been so long in a cage it had forgotten how to fly. But it flew — it circled the small perimeter of the lawn, a creature thrown to the air, its wings beating back the dark for one more turn in the world it hardly remembered before it came back. Ben whistled for it. I watched the bird fly back through the open window to what it knew.

I'd left Virginia before, when I ran away, left by the window in the middle of the night. This time I was leaving in broad daylight. Everyone knew I was going, and no one tried to talk me out of it. They had only been holding on to what they considered a sense of duty — to keep me until I reached the age of consent, and now that I was so close even Reverend Payne didn't dream of getting me to reconsider. The last of the Grovers was about to go, and it seemed to me everyone was relieved.

I waited until the last second to get on the bus in case Ben changed his mind. But there was only Reverend Payne to see me off. He pressed a St. Christopher medal into my palm and told me it was the traveler's protector.

"You can always come back," he said, and the way his gray eyes looked into me I thought he was forgiving me in advance for what he knew I could only think of as capitulation. "Just pick up the phone. You won't have to explain a thing."

I couldn't imagine ever getting to that point. I'd packed my things and stored them in the church basement, put the darkroom equipment back in their original boxes. I would send for all of it when I was ready and that would be the end of any ties I had to Virginia.

As the bus pulled onto the highway I felt myself enter a long black river by which the rest of my family had already made their way into the world. I was following, connecting myself to them by the intricate network of roads, a venous system with a map and clearly marked signs that could bring us in closer proximity or keep us forever blindly passing each other east to west, north to south, the Great Divide somewhere in between.

It took all day to get to the end of Virginia. The west side of the Blue Ridge Mountains followed Highway 91 all the way to Tennessee, and there they took another name, but they were the same slate blue, a tidal wave frozen in midair.

I sat near the front, remembering Mrs. Timberlake's dire warning not to go to the back. For once, she might have been right. Sitting in the back was a boy about my age, and a man who could have been his father. They passed a paper sack back and forth and drank from a bottle concealed inside it. There was something about the two of them that was furtive, trashy, even dangerous. I was determined not to have to use the bathroom so I wouldn't have to go near them.

I felt Ben cross over, along with everyone and everything else in Rappahannock, into recent memory. Ben leaning from my window, Mrs. Timberlake dunking her twice-used tea bag into one more cup of lukewarm water, Reverend Payne's long, almost skeletal hands gripping the steering wheel as he silently mouthed the words of his next sermon. The Coke machine at the general store. The bridge. Ben's hands. Ben's eyes. Angry eyes.

The bus stopped for supper outside of Bristol. I bought a postcard of the Blue Ridge Mountains and sent it to Jack, telling him I was on my way. I said I would call from Phoenix to let him know what time I'd get in. By that time, it would be too late to send me home.

The man and the boy got off at Nashville, and I was glad to see them go. The rest of the trip was terribly dull and quiet except for the constant roar of the asphalt beneath the wheels. What began as a pleasurable hypnosis gradually turned into a relentless rhythm: the noise of the engine, the sameness of the freeway through state after state, the lack of anyone interesting to talk to.

I slept through half of Arkansas. It wasn't until we got into Oklahoma that I started to wake up. We were leaving the green mountains and wetlands behind and pushing into a clearing that went on forever. Hawks drifted, desolate, for long distances on the thermals without once ever flapping their wings. The interstate was a broken line. Whenever we came to a town, construction conveniently forced traffic onto Route 66, which ran through places studded with motels — "Sleep in a Wigwam" one advertised in Henryetta. Each room was an individual wigwam-shaped building with red zigzags painted around it and an air- conditioning unit stuck to its side, ruining its conical symmetry. Cactus Cafes and Pow Wow Diners, Big Chief Gasoline. Everything looked flimsy and slapped together, a place without visible history.

The country outside the window got drier, but the sky grew dark with a storm we headed straight into. The driver pulled off the road when the water flowed so deep and fast over the highway it was no longer a road but a swollen river heading west. Lightning jittered, the wind raked back the scrawny trees on the plains. The whole spectacle was like a movie in Cinemascope, and I felt as if I were seeing a storm for the first time — the gaudy force of weather, not just climate — unimpeded by woods and hills and towns.

I was the only person still on the bus who'd started in Virginia. Most people seemed to ride for short distances — from one city to the next. I was looking forward to the time when I could climb down from that bus and stop moving once and for all. I thought about the homeless people I'd read about on the subways of New York, riding all day and night just to have somewhere to sleep. It could happen to me. If Jack wouldn't take me in, I could be back on this bus for the rest of my life and have nowhere definite to go.

The last day of the journey, the flat plains gave up their relentless reach, and mesas began to break up the horizon. The red rocks and hard blue sky, the gash of pink earth, the maw of canyons and dry riverbeds. It all looked biblical and condemned — the water wrung out, the mountains thrown together like leftover, unglazed clay from a mad potter, blasted and fired by the sun. I watched it all in silence as my heart raced from too much sugary coffee, too little sleep, and a growing apprehension, knowing that the trip was almost over. What had I gotten myself into now? My mind went blank right after the image of myself getting off the bus.

I called Jack first from Albuquerque but got no answer. I called again from Flagstaff, Arizona, and let the phone ring eighteen times before I hung up. When I called from Phoenix, he finally answered.

"Where *are* you?" He didn't sound surprised, or pleased, to hear from me.

"Arizona!" I said in a voice I hardly recognized as my own — so absurdly cheerful. "Phoenix." My legs were shaking. It was all I could do to stand up after all that sitting.

"Why didn't you let me know sooner?"

I couldn't read his voice. I wished I could see his face. "I didn't know sooner," I said, which was not very far from the truth.

The operator asked for more money and I was grateful for the interruption.

"What?"

"I said I don't know." I flipped the coin return lever up and down repeatedly. "I get in at 6:30," I said, then immediately hung up.

I felt sick and exhausted and dirty and nearly deranged. I hadn't had anything but junk food in four days, and my nerves wouldn't even keep that down. The last hundred miles were the longest, and yet they were not long enough. The bus had carried me across the country, through day and night and sleep and dazed wakefulness, across state and county lines. Safely, steadily. And now I was afraid to get off. The idea to come here was ludicrous, risky. I was scared that I had flagrantly disobeyed the gods and now would be punished in some cruel, ironic fashion. Whatever logic I'd used to plan this trip was leaving me in a hurry. And yet I clung to the notion of family, even though the one I was headed for was a long shot. I had no choice but to go for broke, to believe in some wild, windfall luck: that deep down, without knowing it, Jack wanted to see me.

I saw Jack's red pickup in the parking lot as we finally pulled into the Tucson Greyhound station. I stepped slowly off the bus into the kind of heat that comes from an open oven door. I stood behind a woman whose large family swooped in to greet her, shouting in Spanish. The signs in the terminal were in two languages, and I felt as if I'd landed in a foreign country that was hidden inside the United States, a country whose customs I did not know, whose dialect was completely strange.

I could see Jack over their heads. I stood there, teetering. I set my suitcase down.

If we could have embraced the way we did in Virginia, we could have broken the spell. But he clasped me only briefly, and I couldn't get a good look at his eyes. He picked up my suitcase and headed out the door. I had trouble keeping up with him. My legs felt rubbery, as if I'd been at sea a long time and the ground were much more ungiving than I remembered.

He opened the door to the truck. I was glad to sit in a familiar place. I welcomed the scratchy upholstery, the heated vinyl smell of the sun-split dashboard. Aged yellow Styrofoam burst through torn black skin.

The drive to Oracle took just an hour. We skirted the edge of the Santa Catalina Mountains — peaks that seemed newly hacked from the rock — so different from the slow curves of the Blue Ridge. Strange, prickly cactus crowded the slopes, arms like heavy appendages upraised as if a gun were being aimed at them; then they thinned out as we reached the higher elevations. This wasn't the West I had in mind. It was hostile, unwelcoming. And Jack, my long-lost brother, acted as if he wished he'd put me on the next bus out of Tucson. He turned on the radio and strange music filled the cab — whiny accordions and guitars and screechy violins. He turned it up loud, it seemed, so he wouldn't have to talk to me. I wished I could turn back time, make my entrance all over again. I'd blown it, obviously. If only

I'd let him know sooner, then we wouldn't have to be so uncomfortable now.

"What do you have to say for yourself? Whatever it is, it better be good," he said.

"I can't think right now."

"That's awfully convenient, don't you think?" He drove in silence for a while. "What am I supposed to do with you?"

I wanted to say, "I thought you would know," but I didn't dare. I hadn't counted on his being so distant. My dream had been nothing less than stupid, childish — some fairy-tale idea of being taken in. "Well, I don't know what you should do," I said.

It was just like riding in the car with my father — all that silence and the hope and dread of hearing his voice, what he would come up with next. A long story or a bad dream — I never knew. And I didn't know now. I just sat. He just drove. The silence was excruciating.

He turned off the main road and headed south toward Oracle. The terrain changed, began to look and feel more like the Adirondacks, with pine trees and cooler air. It seemed kinder, and I began to relax, just a little.

It was dark when Jack turned in the dirt drive to his house. The headlights showed it to me — an adobe building. A flat roof. A blue door. A black cat on the windowsill.

The house was curved, smooth like a piece of pottery shaped by hand rather than a building nailed together at right angles. A corner fireplace, convex, round as a woman with child. A simple wooden table and chairs painted

yellow and blue. Strings of dried red peppers. I was surprised at how much like a real house it was. What had I
expected — a cave? A hovel of rammed earth with a single,
thin pallet on the dirt floor? It looked like a home. More
than anything I wanted to live there.

He switched a light on in a room off the hall. I walked in
as if in a trance. There was a niche above the single bed
with a candle in it. A nightstand with a small lamp and a jar
full of orange wildflowers.

I stood in the room he'd prepared for me despite his
coldness — or was it only annoyance at being caught off
guard? I sank onto the edge of the bed. I was too tired to
thank him.

"We'll talk in the morning." His voice was softer. "Get
some sleep before you fall over." He closed the door behind
him. I collapsed on the bed, relieved, as if I'd received a stay
of execution. Grateful to be motionless and horizontal,
I fell asleep with the sound of the bus still loud inside
my ears.

When I woke up I didn't know where I was. A ceiling of
peeled logs and the white, smooth walls had suddenly
replaced the dark vaulted attic I used to wake to. Birds
shrieked from the skinny leafless trees as if impaled on the
thorns that protruded from every inch of branch.

Then I heard Jack in the kitchen. The rattle of the kettle
on the stove. Running water. The clink of plates in the dish
drainer. The cat asking to be fed. Morning sounds. Just
hearing them again made me realize how much I missed
them, how in the short time he'd stayed with me I'd gotten
so used to them.

The tile floor met my feet — cool, without a creak. I looked out the window to see what arriving in darkness had hidden from me. Tall blond grass and cactus, the pads shaped like beaver tails and cow tongues studded with stickers as sharp as tacks. A sky so seamlessly blue it looked as if even the sun couldn't crack it open.

I walked slowly, almost tiptoeing down the hallway, into the kitchen. He hadn't heard me yet. He was bent over a small wooden box with a handle. With each turn, the smell of ground coffee grew stronger.

"You look a little better," he said, looking up briefly. "But not much." He actually laughed. "Just kidding."

We took the coffee and some mangoes — a fruit I'd heard of but never seen — outside and sat beneath what Jack called a *ramada*, a roof of branches supported by four uprights. Flecks of sunlight squeezed through and rained down onto the smooth dirt floor, flickering when the tree next to us moved inside a breeze.

I closed my eyes and listened. A jay. Jack sipping his coffee. The cat striding through the dry grass toward us. I felt as if I'd finally walked up to the painting of my real life and that if I could just figure out how to enter it, I'd be home. I went back over everything I had ever wondered or cried about, everything I was sure I had to have, and all of it was less than what I had just come into, like an unexpected inheritance that changed a habit of scrimping into one of wild gratification. I was afraid if I made a sudden move or spoke too soon the image would shatter like a tipped-over mirror.

"What's the cat's name?" I asked.

"It doesn't have one. You give them a name and then they think they belong to you. They start thinking that food only comes in cans."

I stared at the cat and it blinked at me. I wondered what its secret was, if along with remaining nameless it had other strategies for being kept. I was finding out things about Jack now that I'd just as soon not know. If he couldn't give a cat a name, what would he do with me?

We were stalling. I knew he was waiting for me to explain myself, why I'd come, how long I'd be staying.

I thought it might help if I reassured him somehow, so I made up a story. I said that I only needed to stay for a couple of weeks or so, that I was going to live with a distant cousin in California. I did have a distant cousin, but she was in North Dakota the last I knew. An annual Christmas card was the only contact we had. I told Jack I was going to apply to UC Santa Cruz, that I wanted to study marine biology and photography. It was easy — I just used the story my mother would have told and added some embellishments of my own. It sounded plausible enough to me.

"What gave you the idea you could just come here? What gave you the right?"

"I'm your sister," I said, hoping that was an indisputable answer, but I was so flustered it came out sounding more like a question.

I shut my eyes and racked my brain. A few weeks. Hardly enough time to become so much a part of this place that he couldn't imagine me leaving, that he himself would be the one to suggest I stay.

"The least you can do now is help me out," he said,

ignoring my declaration. "I've got a furniture order due in a few days. I'm running behind."

Disappointed and more than a little embarrassed, I followed Jack to his woodshop in back of the house to do my penance, earn my keep. Unfinished chairs hung from the rafters — a thicket of pale blond spokes and arms and legs. A fine accumulation of sawdust had settled over everything. He handed me a sheaf of sandpaper and put me to work sanding the rungs of chairs. I think he expected me to tire easily, or get bored, but I liked the physical motion, the repetition, the transformation from rough to silk. We worked most of the day, broke for lunch, then continued on until late afternoon when the sun finally dipped below the hills and the air began to cool down enough to eat dinner outside. It was almost like the time we spent in Virginia. My fear loosened. I was beginning to settle in.

We got up the next morning at dawn while it was still cool. We made coffee and tortillas. We sat outside under the ramada waiting for the sun to come up behind the Catalina Mountains and the hummingbirds to begin their rounds at the feeders that dangled from the rafters. A large kind of woodpecker hammered on the swamp cooler, and small, clownish birds that looked like some kind of wren screeched and chased each other, running across the flat roof. I wouldn't swear to it, but I don't think he minded my company. I think he might even have been glad for it. In a few days, the rhythm had established itself in me — it was simple, repetitive, reassuring.

I slept deeply for the first time in years — all the way through the night — drifting off when the coyotes started what Jack referred to as the nightly yip-yowl. Through my window I could see them in the moonlight drinking from the tin washtub out by the shed Jack kept filled for them.

At the end of the week we loaded the truck with a few chairs, a cabinet, and a headboard carved with humming-birds. Jack drove to the store where he sold things on consignment. I offered to stay behind, said I just wanted a little time to myself.

Out of curiosity more than anything, I walked down the hall to his room. I'd never even seen the inside except in a quick glimpse through the doorway. He always kept the door closed. As far as I could see, it contained only a double bed in an iron frame and a chair over which he tossed his clothes. Suddenly, I was burning with curiosity. I was sure there was something in that room I had to find.

I opened the door. I stood there for a minute, no longer sure whether I wanted to go in. The room looked stark, almost unlived-in. The bed was so neatly made it looked ironed flat, as if the mattress had never borne his weight. There wasn't a single thing hung on the walls, nothing on the dresser except a pile of small change and a broken comb. I ran my hand across the adobe wall. It was riddled with tiny holes. When I stood back I could see the pattern, because I was looking for it, of faint rectangles, slightly darker than the sun-faded wall. The ghosts of pictures in a gallery that had disappeared, that he'd taken down long ago or taken down because of me? *Playboy* pinups? He didn't seem the type, but still, I wondered. Pictures of an old girl-friend? He'd never once mentioned his love life, past, present, or hopes for the future.

It didn't take long to find what I was looking for. The first place I looked was under his bed after checking the closet shelf. In a way I was disappointed that he was so predictable. A nondescript department store box from Goldwater's, the corners so dry the glue gave way, was the treasure chest. It weighed practically nothing, and because of its lightness didn't seem as if it could contain anything of any real substance or meaning. I carried it into my room, set it on the floor and stared at it, afraid to open it, as if lifting the lid on it would release something that could never be put back. But I couldn't not look, either. I was so close. I could feel the power of what the box contained, humming like a living thing. I lifted the lid.

At first I was disappointed. The usual photographs. A mess of them. Nothing racy. Just Jack and a woman, their arms around each other, their bodies leaning into each other, heads touching. Behind them a campground, a tent, a creek. Pine trees. Huge, egg-shaped boulders. I leafed through them. They all had tiny holes in the corners where the thumbtacks had poked through. It felt strange to be seeing Jack with this woman. He looked happy — broad smile, the lines dropped from his face.

I wasn't expecting to find the elephant — the one Jack won at the fair for me. I hadn't even realized it was missing. But seeing it there, hidden in a box beneath his bed made me wonder about him all over again. He was someone who wouldn't stoop so low as to give a cat a name, but he held on to the elephant, and what's more, kept them hidden.

At the bottom of the box I found pictures of my father — little strips containing him alone. Jack had systematically

snipped my father out of pictures he'd once been a part of.
Again, my brother was a contradiction. He'd taken the
trouble to cut and save — I would have thought that throwing them in a fire would have been more his style.

I was sorry I'd found his secrets — they were so small,
really, in the grand scheme of things. It made him less mysterious and more so, more understandable in a painful,
human way. But there was no way to talk about it without
admitting that I'd trespassed. He'd already let me into his
home and now I'd broken into his room. The problem was,
I didn't know what to do with the knowledge, how to stop
it from coloring the way I saw him after that — no longer
compelling, just wounded and ordinary. I put everything
back in the box, back the way I'd found it.

At the end of my second week Jack said that since I wouldn't
be there much longer we should take a couple of days off,
go on a backpacking trip to Aravaipa Canyon. He had me
wear my worst sneakers because the trail was in the middle
of Aravaipa Creek. I'd never heard of such a hike.

We drove through San Manuel and headed south along
Aravaipa Creek as it wound its way through a valley. Skinny
cattle grazed the dry scrub. Everything looked lean and
leached out for miles, but then the land began to change.
The creek seemed to come alongside the road from out of
nowhere, then kept crisscrossing it. Jack gunned the engine
and we plunged through the water, sending up a great fan
of spray that shot up all around us.

Jack yelled for me to hang on as we surged up the bank.
The truck fishtailed in the deep sand and fought its way for-

ward. We got just enough traction to keep moving, and I grabbed onto the windwing frame as we gained speed — slowing down would have gotten us instantly stuck. The road didn't get any better until we pulled into the trailhead parking lot. It was a weekday, and we had the place to ourselves.

Red rock cliffs rose above the green canopy of cottonwoods, and above them, a crown of blue sky. The path followed the creek for a while, but the further we went, the narrower the canyon grew until we were slogging right through the water with the canyon walls flanking us.

We walked for nearly two hours until we came to a flat, grassy bank wide enough to set up camp. When he lifted the pack off me, I felt so light I thought I'd float straight up into the sky. Something about the trees and the canyon wall and the boulders looked familiar, but I couldn't place it right away.

I gathered some kindling while Jack dug a fire pit with a trowel he'd brought. I watched with a great deal of envy that he knew how to do all these things. In a way, he was more like my mother than like my father. I was determined that I would learn from him.

"How many times have you been here?" I asked.

"Just once, twice maybe. I forget." He fiddled with the fire. The way his eyebrows drew together gave the opposite impression — as if it pained him to remember. "I came with a friend," he added, then asked me to get more kindling. "You got the wrong kind before — too green. What's a girl's education coming to these days? Didn't they ever teach you in the Scouts?" He hacked away at a dead branch with a small hatchet. A pile of shavings accumulated at his feet.

"So, do you have a private life or what?" I asked.

"Do you?"

"I asked you first."

"Here," he said, sweeping his arm wide with the hatchet still in his hand, including the campsite, the trees, me, "is my private life. Camping with a relative. I've been reduced to this."

I couldn't tell if he was kidding or not. He sounded sarcastic, almost whiny. Not exactly what I'd call serious, but his face was as set as stone.

"Who was she?"

"She *is* Silvia, still. She *was*, for lack of a better word, my girlfriend. She went back to Mexico. End of story."

"This exact same place — you were here with her?"

He ignored the question, but I knew. It was the boulders I recognized from the snapshot in the box beneath his bed. He busied himself making dinner — rigged up a spit with forked sticks, just like in cowboy movies. He might be cryptic, but he was handy. I was amazed he knew how to do "man-things." Our father could quote Keats and Wordsworth to a fare-thee-well but was useless with a hammer.

Jack skewered some frozen meat we'd brought with us, now completely thawed, and turned it on the spit. I wrapped corn in foil, placed it in the coals.

"Don't you want to know about my private life?" I asked, as a joke, to ease us back into conversation again.

He blew on the coals to make the fire hotter, didn't answer.

"I don't have a boyfriend. Not now." I answered what I assumed should be a logical first question.

He finally looked at me. "You will." When he took his eyes off me again, I felt his prediction falter, too.

"Why do you say that?"

"Didn't anyone ever tell you you're pretty?"

My heart stopped. No one had ever said such a thing to me before.

"Your former boyfriend — didn't he tell you?"

"Don't you think that's a little personal?" I had to laugh. "See — it's so much easier to ask questions than to answer them."

Birds trilled as they flew in and out of nests tucked into the steep canyon walls. The sun went below the rim of the world.

"I've never been camping in my life," I said, trying to change the subject. "Did he take you — you know, before he left?"

"Who?"

"Our father." I must have turned red with embarrassment. It sounded formal, like something one said in church.

"He wasn't the camping type — you should know that."

"Yeah, well, one less happy little memory to haunt you."

I was surprised at the bitterness in my own voice, the simultaneous sharp, clear picture I had of my father standing waist deep in the river, my mother trying to coax him further. The white mystery of his bare chest, the dark swatch of hair between his breasts, the sun in his eyes, the way he raised his arm to fend off the light, to shield himself from my mother, who kicked up water as she swam away from him. I had the eerie feeling, or maybe it was just wishful thinking, that Jack could see inside of me, that my memories could also be his. I imagined that scene in the river projected in black and white upon a sheet hung on a wall, the flickering images. I wanted to show him everything — everything he'd missed.

We ate the chicken and the corn with our hands and washed the fat from our fingers in the creek afterward. I began to feel a deep contentment, a sense that everything was right, of not wanting to change a single thing. The stars began to sharpen into focus, a few at a time. The moon rose over the rim. Unimpeded by the veil of humidity, it threw blue shadows everywhere. The night was every bit as bright as a cloudy day in Virginia. The water moved slow and bright as mercury. I wanted to be in it.

I ran hopping across the sharp gravel. I stripped to my underwear and splashed in.

"Last one in!" I called over my shoulder.

Jack ambled over with a cup of tea and stood there on the bank while I splashed and flounced. The shining ripples and eddies were dizzying.

I skimmed the water hard and fast with the side of my hand, sending up a spray like slivers of ice.

He took another long sip. It steamed from the cup. "Can't."

"Can't or won't?"

"Can't swim."

"Who said anything about swimming? Anyway, I'm not about to let you drown — you're all I've got left." As soon as

I said it I wanted to take it back. Why couldn't I just think things through before I opened my mouth? If I didn't watch it, I'd end up pushing him away, pushing myself right out of the house.

Some ragged clouds the color of old bruises swam across the moon, dimming the light. Jack took off his T-shirt and shorts and dropped them on the gravel. His underwear looked white as a truce flag moving in the half dark. He waded in to his waist, sending little waves folding toward me. He stopped. The water settled flat again.

I waded toward him, each step slowed by the gravity of water. I had the feeling that if I moved too fast he'd bolt. I came up alongside him and stretched my arms out underwater. "Now lean back — I've got you."

"This is silly."

I thought of the way Ben had just walked right into the river without blinking an eye. For a second, I almost started to miss him, but stopped myself.

"It's all right. Nobody's watching," I said. "I've got you."

He leaned back across my arms. His head went back, his feet came up and my arms caught him under his waist. He floated in front of me, hair streaming dark in the water, his eyes taking in the sky. I turned slowly in a circle, his body like a long blade stirring the water. He stretched his arms out, spread eagle. He closed his eyes. It would have been so easy to lean down and kiss him. He wouldn't have seen me coming, would simply have felt it happen. My hands wanted to move down his spine, to touch his face, for him to touch me back. I wanted to be looked into, surrounded by someone who knew and cared for me. But more than that,

I wanted to be the one in the water, leaning back against the certainty of his arms, held safely in the water that seemed so harmless but could pull a person, like my mother's sister, Emma, completely under.

I stopped turning. He opened his eyes. I took my arms away. He started to sink, then his feet touched bottom. Far to the north I thought I heard thunder.

Birds that had been roosting, invisible in the cottonwoods, shot out of the branches and scattered in all directions.

"What spooked them?" I asked.

Jack lurched to a standing position. "Bobcat, maybe." We peered at the shadows along the bank, looking for something moving. Nothing did. And then we heard it again — a distant, dull roar.

Jack started yelling. "Shit. Oh God. Run!"

The water surged. Confused, I lunged toward the nearest bank.

"What is it?" I yelled, thinking he was right behind me. Then I looked across the creek where Jack stood yelling, one hand cupped around his mouth, the other arm jerking, pointing upward. Then he turned and scrambled up the hill.

I had no idea what was happening. It hadn't even been raining. I crashed through a thicket and clawed my way on all fours up a steep hillside. The roar grew deafening below me.

Finally, when I'd gone as high as I could go, I turned and looked back.

A wall of churning water shot through the canyon, roiling with branches and rocks and entire trees. I watched our packs swallowed whole and swept away. I started shivering. I couldn't see Jack anywhere. I sat huddled on the hillside, dressed only in my underwear. The water kept coming. It rose higher. Bushes torn from their roots rushed away. A cloud that had covered the moon rolled back and the moon opened its eye again, as if astonished at what it saw below.

The water found its level, and then almost immediately, it started to subside, as if an enormous drain had been opened downstream. I had no idea how much time had passed. The moon was gone below the rim when the creek shrank back to a swollen version of itself. There was nothing to do but wait.

Near dawn, the sky came up innocent and blue. I made my way down the hill. Jack was shouting from the opposite bank — I couldn't hear words, just his voice. I shouted back.

The banks were a muddy mess strewn with debris, but the creek itself looked fairly calm. Except for its muddy brown color, you'd never know it was capable of sweeping away everything in its path.

Jack started walking downstream. We moved parallel along the ruptured streambanks for more than a mile until I found a place where I could safely cross over. Jack grabbed my hand to pull me up the bank. I could feel him shivering.

"I should have known," he said as he let go of my hand. He kept talking. He was wound up; he kept trying to explain. "I should have heard it, but my ears were underwater when I was floating. It happens this time of year," he said, his voice shaking from shock and cold. He sounded angry with himself. We stumbled over rocks and strewn branches. It was a slow, painful progression. "It can be storming somewhere else and pick up speed as it moves north. I checked before we left. No forecast for rain in this part of Arizona. Even so, I should have been more careful."

"It's not your fault."

"I shouldn't have come in the water. I would have heard it sooner."

I felt ashamed on top of everything else, as if I had somehow caused it. The gods had sent a warning. Next time they wouldn't be so lenient.

It took twice as long walking out as coming in since we'd lost our shoes. We emerged at the trailhead, limping like shipwrecked people in our underwear. Luckily, Jack had a spare key hidden in the wheel well. All I remember after that was lying across the front seat, my head on his lap. He'd put a blanket over me that smelled of piñon. I slept all the way home.

I fell into bed and didn't dream a thing. I woke several times — once I thought I heard the phone ring. Each time I felt damp leaves on the pillow. My hair still smelled like rain. I knew it was the storm that would be remembered and talked about, that there would never be any mention of how I'd held him safely in the water before the whole world came crashing down and the river intervened.

When I woke once again because I had to pee, but the headlights of a car swept across the wall of my room. I heard feet cross the gravel. There was no knock on the door. It opened and closed, quietly.

I got out of my bed. I was so thoroughly awake my ears rang as I listened. I pushed my door ajar, inched down the hall until I could see into the living room. It was dark, but light from the setting moon slowly revealed her shape.

When my eyes grew accustomed to the dark I could see Jack, or at least his silhouette, in the overstuffed chair by the window. He sat there, perfectly still. The shape of a woman in a long skirt moved through the room, straight toward him, in no hurry. When she got to the chair, she leaned her hip against it, then settled on its arm. Jack's hand circled her waist, pulled her onto his lap, and she curled up like she had come to hear a story. As far as I could tell, they sat there without saying a single word, without moving.

He rose up from the chair, still holding her. Moonlight grazed one shoulder, one hip. He was completely naked. He undressed her, one article of clothing at a time, beginning with whatever she wore on her feet, then working his way up.

"*Querida*," I thought I heard her say, as her blouse dropped softly to the floor.

He picked her up, and her legs wrapped around his hips. She was so small she couldn't have weighed much more than a child. I closed my eyes and leaned my back against the cool adobe behind me. I pressed my palms flat against the wall, holding on to the house. I could hear them breathing, and somehow without my conscious thought, my body began to breathe in rhythm with them. Faster, then something like a painful moan. She let out one sharp little cry — it might as easily have been a bird.

I got back to my room feeling my way down the hall. My eyes refused to open. I grasped the door frame of my room and let go reluctantly, groping for the bed that was somewhere in front of me. I rolled onto it. Jealous? Relieved? I thought about yelling, about faking a bad dream so he would put her down and come running, but I was wide awake, and I couldn't utter a sound. I was not willing to risk the possibility of being drowned out by that other sound — that song from Silvia that only she could sing.

In the morning she was gone. Jack was asleep in his room. Except for a plain silver bracelet on the floor next to the chair, she could have been someone I dreamed.

I saw in Jack the shadow of our father forming — an indefinite shape outlined by longing, by his desire for Silvia. For Silvia had come back, as if from the dead, and was now a force to be reckoned with. He wrote her name over and over again on the yellow pad by the phone. He began to make what I thought of as a marriage bed — he said when she came back from Mexico the next time she would stay for good. He believed her because she'd never said such a thing before, made such a promise to him. His voice grew soft, almost conspiratorial when he spoke to her on the phone. He read the international weather in the paper just to know what kind of climate touched her there.

I'd never seen him take so much care with a piece of furniture. All the other things he'd made, he never knew who would end up sitting in them, but he made Silvia's bed as if he could already see her lying there, arms spread wide across its double width, her feet nowhere near its edge.

The next time Jack went into town I went with him. Oracle was not much bigger than Rappahannock. It had a post

office and a general store, a cafe. Huge boulders that had
spilled out of the mountains long ago were scattered and
jumbled throughout the town.

We took the furniture into the back entrance of the "By
Hand" shop, and a man the size of a bear standing on small,
almost dainty feet greeted us. Jack introduced me to Filiberto. "My half-sister," Jack mumbled. "Matty."

Filiberto smiled. He shook my hand. "Everybody's half
something — I'm half Yaqui Indian, half Jewish. Go figure."

I couldn't tell how old he was, though I guessed he was
nearly forty. His hair was long and black, streaked with
gray, tied at the back of his neck with red string.

"She's too pretty to be related to you, Jack. Where have
you been hiding her — I didn't even know you had a family.
Well," he said, still holding my hand, "maybe with you here
you can drag him into town more often. He's going to forget how to talk if he keeps up that sorry excuse for a social
life he's been having."

I looked at Jack. His face showed no definable expression, but the muscles in his jaw worked constantly.

"You ever hear from Silvia?" Filiberto asked.

"Just the other day."

A short silence followed that nobody seemed to want to
tamper with, as if we were honoring the memory of someone recently dead.

"I'm surprised," he said, then wrote Jack a check for
what he'd sold from the previous delivery, which had been
everything Jack had brought him.

After that, Jack let me take the truck into town every

few days to get the groceries. I lingered there, walking the single street, peering into the half-dozen shop windows, and stopping for coffee at the Linda Vista Cafe.

Filiberto came into the cafe one afternoon as I sat there flipping through the Tucson morning newspaper. He asked if he could join me. I was surprised that he remembered my name after such a brief introduction and was relieved to have someone to talk to.

"It's a pretty slow life in this town," he said, nodding at the newspaper. "Not like in the big city, if you call Tucson a city."

"I came from a place a lot slower than this."

"Virginia, right?"

"Yeah."

"Oh, man. Dixie."

"They even play that as the anthem before the movies, with a rebel flag projected on the screen. Believe me, everybody stands."

Filiberto shook his head. "They still haven't given up, have they? They still want that grand old plantation monarchy. The black waiting hand and foot on the white."

"I haven't even seen a black person here; and the Indians — I thought they'd be everywhere."

"They are, they're just invisible if you're looking for the wrong picture — you know, warbonnets, painted ponies, all that bullshit. They're playing bingo after work. They're trying to pay their bills, raise their kids. They're living their lives, and that's not the kind of thing tourists want to see — it's a long way from being an attraction."

I thought of how I'd put Jones in the public eye just by

taking his picture at the right moment, and how since I'd left Virginia I'd moved to the sidelines. My camera wasn't seeing much of anything these days — I hadn't even picked it up since I'd arrived.

"Where's Jack today — holed up in his lair?"

"He's busy working on a bed for Silvia — the woman you asked him about."

"So that worked out."

"I guess. Maybe he won't even have to deliver the bed. Maybe she'll just move right in and start sleeping in it."

"He's a little loco — he's kept to himself ever since I've known him, almost five years now, but when he gets fixated on something, watch out."

"Like Silvia?"

Filiberto rolled his eyes. "I'll never know how they got together in the first place, or back together now. They met at the Norteño Festival in Tucson — Jack's a great dancer. It was like that fairy tale — at the stroke of midnight he turned into himself again, which is to say he stood still. But she kept moving. His pace — this is what I think — is what drove her crazy. She acted like he'd misrepresented himself. Then she started seeing some other guy in a band, went on the road with him back to Nogales." He raised his hand to the waitress who sailed over to us with a steaming pot. She poured him a refill, but I shook my head and held my hand over my cup. "Jack followed her, but he wasn't gone long. When he came back he just holed up out there at the house. I thought he'd never come out again. One time when I went out there he was sitting in a big easy chair he'd dragged out into the yard, just sitting back, taking a shot of tequila. He had a portable record player and was listening to these Spanish lessons. He didn't just repeat the lines after the woman on the record. He shouted them. It was like he thought if he could learn her language he could talk her into coming back."

I wondered where all that shouting had gone.

"Well I guess it's good that he's got something else to be fixated on — you know what they say about idle hands."

"Devil's workshop." I laughed. "It makes me picture a woodshop lined with skulls and candles."

"And a fire in a dark forge, constantly burning. And *Phantom of the Opera* music."

For the first time since I'd been in Arizona I laughed hard and long, and when I did he said, "I think you should do that more often. Looks good on you. I'll bet you've been serious all your life — you come from a serious kind of family."

He looked at his watch. "I gotta get back — stop by later if you want."

I couldn't wait more than half an hour — there wasn't anything else to do to kill time. The bell on the door clanged as I went in. Filiberto was standing behind the counter rubbing oil into a fiddle. He looked glad to see me. "Look at this," he said, holding up the instrument. "Beautiful thing." He held up its slender body. Its sound holes were cut in the shape of birds.

I ran my hand down one of its symmetrical sides where the wood drew inward like a waist, then flared to a hip, then finally tapered to a point where the strings had their source.

"An old Apache man named Henry Loco makes these."

"You play?" I asked.

"Not really. Sometimes."

Filiberto lifted the instrument to his chin and rested his beard on the blond wood. He drew the bow across the strings — a little hesitant at first, then the tune pulled him forward — into a jaunty, crazy waltz. I don't know what got into me. I took off my sneakers — wanted to feel that wooden floor beneath my bare feet. I started moving to it, slid slowly around the room, weaving in and out of the tables and shelves of pottery and stacks of blankets and Jack's chairs. My feet flew over the smooth floor. I circled back around to him and we danced together, the fiddle between us. I felt silly and almost happy. I felt graceful when his eyes were on me. Then I knocked into a table of pottery and sent a vase crashing to the floor. As I jumped back I cut my foot on one of the shards. Filiberto dropped the fiddle and came to me as I stood there on one foot like a heron. He made me sit down in one of Jack's chairs. Blood trickled into his palm.

"I've got bandages. Stay put."

I pressed my thumb hard into the wound to stop the flow. It didn't really hurt, and I was more embarrassed than anything else. Filiberto came back with cotton balls and alcohol and went to work. Before he put the bandage on he lifted my foot and kissed the arch. I was so surprised I nearly jerked it away.

"Sorry," he said. "Can't help it." He wrapped gauze over the heel, crisscrossing at the ankle and tying it until it looked like a white sandal.

"I should get home."

"You could stay," he said. "Or you could come with me to Alaska. I close the store every September."

I could feel Filiberto wanting me, the warmth and pressure of the idea. And I knew I didn't want him back, at least not yet. But Filiberto didn't push any harder.

"Crazy idea," he said. "But I had to ask." He walked me to the truck, held the door open, and made a deep bow, thanking me for the dance. "Your slipper," he said, holding out my bedraggled shoe.

When Jack heard the truck he came running out of the house before I even cut the engine. All the lights were off in the house.

"Where the hell have you been?"

"Sorry," I said. "I lost track of time." Then I added, somewhat defensively, pushing back at his voice, "I was at Filiberto's. Dancing on tables and breaking dishes," I said, hoping to get him to laugh.

"Jesus Christ," he said, seeing my bandaged foot as I got out of the truck. "Look at you."

"What do you care!" I cried.

He looked surprised and then confused, and then the last flicker of anger flowed across his features and left a stern mask behind.

I stood my ground. He stood his, though the place each of us claimed was shaky.

The headlights were still on, and a flurry of moths darted frantically in the cones of light. He shut them off, extinguishing all those wings with one stroke.

Jack's fist rose, then fell, slammed into the fender with a

ringing thud. I limped past him and then broke into a lopsided run into the house. I slammed the door of my room
and sat on my bed, shaking. I heard his steps come down
the hall, pause at my door. He stayed there a long time. He
didn't knock. He went into his room. The whole house
shook as he shut the door hard behind him.

That night I dreamed about my father, and in the dream
I felt so happy to see him. He wrote poems and read them
to me, but then the police came to the door with one of the
poems and said they found it next to a murdered woman.
He came home after dark and read me another poem — a
love poem — and when he got up to leave I knew he was
going out to kill someone again. I tried to stop him, but I
couldn't. I woke up yelling and sweating and terrified. I had
no idea where I was. And then Jack came running into my
room. I was shaking so hard I could barely breathe. He
pulled me up and held me. I felt his bare back beneath my
hands. My cheek rested against the soft fur of his chest. He
stroked my hair.

I felt jangled, mixed up, stirred up, aroused. He stayed
for a few minutes — two or twenty, I couldn't tell — then
finally said, "Close your eyes now."

I closed them for several seconds, then opened them
again and saw what he didn't want me to see — his half
erect penis as he quickly turned, his naked form hurrying
from the room.

Jack and I drove into Tucson two days later to meet Silvia at
the Norteño Festival. I wasn't sure I wanted to see her. He'd
thrown himself into at least half a dozen home improve-

ment projects — building shelves, fixing the back door, which never closed all the way, cleaning out closets. I could just picture my room turning into her study. Silvia was filling up the house before she even got there, and all I could think of was that my days were surely numbered.

Della walks every day as usual but she's slowing down. The rocky slope becomes an obstacle she pits herself against; the hill, it seems, is winning.

This morning I pray for rain. If the weather changes, then maybe the spell will be broken. Lightning and thunder could tear the sky apart, the rain push away the seal of humid air. It's all a tease. The clouds that look so promising never build to critical mass, and what builds inside myself, fitful and roiling, never comes to much.

I don't want the noise of the outside world to come in. Now, since it refuses to rain, since memories stir everything up and nothing settles again, I turn on the radio. I want to drown everything out. And there's nothing better than accordions for complete auditory distraction.

A Hermosillo station with a signal so strong it bowls over everything in Southern Arizona is playing *cumbia* — perfect. For a few minutes I even dance to it, all by myself on the patio. But the gods have sent me this particular music to mock me, and I go, kicking and screaming toward a night I wish I were too embarrassed to remember.

The streets of South Tucson were lit with the small neon *cerveza* signs in restaurants and the rigged extension-cord lights of food vendors from vans moored in corner lots selling *birria, horchata,* tacos, snow cones. Jack and I parked on a quiet side street where people sat in aluminum chairs on porches. Christmas lights were strung loosely along the roof lines, and handmade grottoes, housing the Virgin of Guadalupe or the Virgin Mary, glowed with the rippling yellow-red light of dozens of votive candles.

We walked toward the music. In a few blocks we were in the middle of it, the air thick and sweet with mesquite smoke from carne asada searing over grills made from oil drums. Women made tortillas, softly slapping the dough until it stretched thin as skin, as big as a dinner plate, then they draped it across the lid of the hot griddle to brown.

It looked to me as if people in South Tucson did their living on the outside in the midst of music and cooking fires and color — all of it crisscrossed, stitched together by the constant music, the ragged trails of children running and shouting. Rappahannock's church picnics seemed paltry in comparison, and even where Jack lived was remote from any lives except our own. But even within the city of Tucson there was an irrefutable border, with more differences than mere language keeping people apart. The Mexican people weren't black, in terms of color, but they were dark and separate just the same.

Jack seemed at ease here. We ate carne asada tacos drenched in red sauce, and Jack gave me some of his beer to wash the fire down. My lips burned with pepper. I couldn't see the stage but could hear accordions and violins and guitars tuning up when the band changed. We walked down the crowded street to a small park where a platform rose above the grass, sheltered by trees.

The men in the band wore cowboy hats and serious expressions as they bent to their instruments, coaxing an odd, rollicking music from the wood and brass. The crowd began to shuffle, then broke into pairs. Jack looked around for Silvia. "She said she'd meet us here by the stage," he said. He couldn't stop scanning the crowd and looking at his watch — she was late. He was nervous as a cat in a new place. Here was my brother, eager to meet his lover, afraid, probably, that she wouldn't show. Here was his sister, praying she wouldn't. Finally, I couldn't stand his fidgeting any longer. I took his hand and pulled him into the swirl of dancers. Almost as soon as we started the song was over, and we stood there like two kids on a first date, not knowing whether to sit this one out or wait for the next song to begin. I could feel him wanting to escape. He scanned the crowd again, and again didn't find her. "One more," I said. "Come on — please?" He shook his head but I took a step toward him, moved his hand to my waist, held my right hand out for him to take.

The next song came on slower. Violins cried, an accordion played an aching melody. A woman got up on stage and poured her dark, risky voice straight into the microphone. I watched my feet trying to match Jack's steps, but it was a mirror, all backward. All I wanted was to be a good dancer, to move easily with him.

"Stop watching your feet — close your eyes." He was leading me now.

When I closed my eyes the music seemed louder. I tried
to imagine I was floating in a river. Like Ben, I felt that
being suspended in water was the only place in the world
where my body had any grace at all. I tried to let myself be
carried along by the current of music and other dancers. I
felt Jack's body — the little signals it gave when he was
about to turn or change direction. I moved closer to him,
felt our nearly six-foot height matched, shoulder to shoulder, knee to knee. His hand rested on the small of my back,
guiding me. I began to sense how he would move next.
There was a pattern to it, a pattern I could learn after all.
The woman's voice soared as if her heart would break. I
could feel the song coming to an end, and I didn't want it
to. I didn't know the words, but I didn't have to — the song
was about love, having it and losing it and wondering if
you'll ever get it back again. As the last note hung in the air,
he began to pull away. I held him tighter. I closed my eyes
again. Then I knew what I wanted, and I didn't care who
saw it. I kissed him. Right on the mouth. For half a second
he returned that kiss, or at least it felt that way. If he'd held
on a second longer I would have pushed past the fence of
his teeth with my tongue. I opened my eyes. Behind him, a
woman still in her man's embrace smiled at me. *"Besa,
besa,"* she said softly, then opened her red lips and laughed.

He looked incredulous, even helpless. He backed away.

I was absolutely sure the gods were going to get me
now.

He raised his hand as he looked over the top of my head.
I turned around. It was Silvia, by the stage — I recognized
her from her picture. She was carrying something in her

hand — a stick wrapped in crepe paper with a decorated egg on the end. She held it toward me. I thought she was giving it to me. I held out my hand, but she raised it to strike me on the head. I closed my eyes, heard her laughter, felt something break against my skull. I expected yoke to run down my face. Instead, a cloud of confetti showered down on me from the broken blue shell.

Jack wanted to leave right away, which was a relief to me. The last thing I wanted to do was watch them dance. Silvia looked disappointed, but she let him have his way. The three of us rode back to Oracle in Jack's truck. I scrunched down into the seat, folding my arms across my chest. I was trapped against the door, fenced in by her right thigh, which was about a foot shorter than my own.

"So," she said. "How long are you visiting for?"

I stole a look at her. She smiled.

"Why?"

She shrugged. "Just wondering."

She smiled again, but I didn't trust it. I was not about to confide in her.

"You're a lot alike," she said, glancing first at me, then at Jack. I couldn't read her eyes or her mind. "Tough, silent types." She laughed, rested her hand on Jack's shoulder. "My brothers and I spend a lot of time jumping up and down and yelling at each other." Her hands flew in front of her, illustrating her words, her fingers illuminated briefly by the headlights of oncoming cars. "My whole family is loud — you don't have to guess what kind of mood anybody's in." She looked at Jack. "Our fights are over in ten minutes."

Here she was, lumping Jack and me together. Didn't she know we didn't grow up together, that there was no reason in the world we should be anything alike, barely reason at all for us to physically resemble one another? "Night and day," I said.

"What?"

"Jack and I — you just can't see it yet. But you will." Even I didn't know what I meant by that. I only wanted to act as if I had privileged information. Jack squirmed in his seat. And no wonder — if I hadn't been filled with such blind indignation I would have seen it, even in the dim lights from the dash. My brother was a man in love, and that kind of love had no room for me. My kiss lingered, not sweet like hers, but a brash claim — the desperate gesture of one about to be spurned. Jealous sister — how I hated becoming that — pushing my luck until I was banished from the kingdom forever.

Before we all went to bed, I locked myself in the bathroom. I couldn't resist snooping. I turned on the tap so that the running water would cover the sound of the zipper on her toiletries case.

Cotton swabs, prescription bottles, cream in a jar, three different shades of lipstick. A big blue compact, which I promptly opened.

Inside, a small rubber dome dusted with talc, pale as a mushroom cap. I snapped it shut, tried not to think about the fact that it had been inside her, keeping my brother's sperm at bay, that it was not inside her now. What was she doing — trying to get pregnant? I'd seen a diaphragm — in my mother's purse, and when I had told Carolyn she was only too glad to induct me into the world of sex and its implements. "It's birth control," Carolyn had said secretively. "Doesn't your mother tell you anything?" Then Carolyn added, raising her eyebrows as she said, "I wonder why she takes it with her everywhere." I didn't want to think about it then, but now I wondered if my mother had had a lover she met in secret, if she had been tired of her housewife life hitched up to her like a plow, a thing so heavy it would make her put that compact in her purse, get in the car and drive to some dead-end road by the river whose slow rush would almost hide the sounds she made with the lover who met her there. It seemed possible. For the first time I wondered if her Virginia Beach trips had been to meet him, and I tried to imagine what he looked like, if he had finally been a man her own age, someone she could be freer with, unlike my father who was twenty years older, caught in the grip of ancient, indisputable mythology. I felt almost claustrophobic in that tiny room, crowded with possibilities.

I woke at first light and slipped out of the house to watch the sun come up. I heard a door close. Silvia came out to the ramada and began scattering birdseed. I wasn't aware that Jack even kept any. Obviously, she knew where everything was in the house. I watched her — the way she flung out her arm, the way the seed scattered like rain. The way the birds came to take from her. She spilled some of it into my hands.

"Do you know the names of the birds?" she asked, sweeping her arm to indicate them all.

I shook my head and threw the seed just to have something to do with my hands.

Jack came out the back door with two cups of coffee. He avoided my eyes completely. He handed one to Silvia, then went back into the house.

A bird whistled loudly. I looked at Silvia.

"Curved-bill thrasher. That," she said, pointing to a bush where I was certain a cardinal had just landed, "is a pyrrhuloxia. And this," she said, touching my forearm gently, "is your heart, right there on your sleeve."

I looked down to where she pointed, half expecting to see a red heart like an ace, Poe's "Tell-Tale Heart," a dead giveaway.

I raised my eyes to meet hers. She was not accusing me. I could feel that. Her look was not the same as Carolyn's shaming stare. Still, I was ready to deny anything she said. She knew. Maybe more than I did. I felt as exposed as a single spared tree in a clear-cut forest, enveloped for the first time by the full influence of light and wind.

Even so, I could not stop myself. "You may know a lot about birds, but you don't know shit about me." I flung the last of the seed as far as I could. "What are you doing here anyhow? Why did you come back?"

"He wanted a second chance. He asked me to marry him."

I didn't expect a straight answer, but I had to keep going — I was in the thick of it now. "What did you tell him?"

She looked at me curiously, as if I weren't any kind of a sister since I didn't even know my own brother's wedding plans. "I said I'd think about it."

"And?"

"And I'm still thinking. I'll let you know as soon as I do. OK? You don't have to pack your bags — the jury's still out."

I stalked across the dry grass of the backyard and kept on going — not anywhere in particular, but just to be moving. I climbed over a fence and soon found myself in a mesquite *bosque* densely populated with cattle. They were huge, dusty, beyond bovine. These weren't East Coast dairy cows, but western range cattle — stringy looking, intense, capable of stampede at the least provocation. But when I ran at them, they only scattered slowly, as if I were no more than a bothersome puppy. I shouted, brandished a stick. One of the steers bucked slightly, then took that opportunity to shit profusely — a green mudpie steamed at my feet. I gave up. I threw the stick down. The cattle watched me go. Every once in a while I turned around to find them motionless, staring, waiting for me to leave their field before they started eating again.

A letter arrived from Rappahannock on church stationery — Reverend Payne's cursive script flowed briefly across the beige paper that had sat so long in a desk drawer in the rectory its edges were brown as parchment. Church correspondence must have been minimal — the annual report to the diocese in Richmond, a formal thank-you to the woman from Delaplane who donated new hymnals. Mrs. Timberlake had had a stroke and lost her speech along with her memory, Reverend Payne wrote, and was living in a nursing home in Culpeper. He said my things were still in the church basement, and that, not to worry, there was always room for me at his house. "I hope this letter finds you well, and that it will reassure you that even in the midst of these dire, unforeseen circumstances with which you already are so familiar, you still have a place in the world to call home."

I handed Jack the letter. I thought about Mrs. Timberlake, robbed of her singing voice, her clear channel to God. I wondered if her memory of me had been erased in an instant, the slate of her mind cleared even of my name.

"I'm not going back there," I said before Jack even had time to finish the letter. We looked at each other across that piece of paper.

He folded the letter into its envelope and handed it back to me. "I thought you were going to California."

I'd all but forgotten that story. Our eyes locked. I was torn between defending a thin lie and just giving in to the truth, but I couldn't seem to do either. I shrugged and looked away like a nine-year-old confronted with the evidence of petty theft.

"Well?"

I felt as if I were on trial and wasn't even sure what I was being charged with. "You're my *family!*" I yelled at him, as if I had every right to be indignant. This was not the way I'd planned it. I think I'd assumed all along that he knew me well enough to know what I wanted. He'd prepared a room for me, hadn't he? We'd escaped the flood together — these were not *vacation* things. And besides — I'd kissed him, and I believe that for a second he'd kissed me back. Neither of us had been struck down. We'd survived the unthinkable.

Silvia had even seen it and decided somehow that I was
more to be pitied than scorned.

"Go ahead," he said, anger raising his voice against me.
"Do what the Grovers always do. Don't let anybody in on
your plans. Drop the bomb and run."

I made myself walk deliberately across the yard and into
the woodshop. I jerked the light on and the bulb swung, its
flustered light sweeping across the room. I grabbed the first
thing I saw — a pair of needlenose pliers — and I went at the
headboard of Silvia's marriage bed. I gripped the pliers hard,
turned them upside down in both hands, and dug the point
in, dragging it through the wood. When I was finished, there
was a ragged gash the length of my arm scratched into the
bed. I threw the pliers down. I felt Jack come up behind me. I
stood there, staring at the bed, shuddering. It looked like the
brazen graffiti left behind by a vandal.

"I didn't mean to," I whispered.

His voice rose until he was shouting. "You don't mean a
lot of things, but you do them anyway."

Silvia walked in on us, a bemused look on her face until
she saw the headboard. "So you *do* know how to fight." I
couldn't tell if she was talking to him or to me, or both of us
together. "You just don't fight fair."

Everything was going wrong. Jack was going to wind up
hating me before he threw me out — I was sure of it.

"Stay out of this," he said, his jaw tightly clenched.

But she was enjoying it. It seemed she'd forgotten the
headboard already, was now enjoying the spectacle of Jack
in a rage.

"Hey, *mijito*," she said, teasing. "*Qué bueno!*"

He looked as if he would shatter his own teeth if he bit down any harder.

"Where's your father when you need him?" she laughed.

What did she know about him? She seemed to know everything — she had a future with Jack, and she already had his history, all the details and chronology. Now she'd brought my father into it, where he didn't belong.

She parked herself on one of his unfinished chairs. Her legs didn't even reach the floor. "Go ahead," she said to Jack. "Call him."

Jack let her have it. "And then what — bring him to my house so he can sneak off in the middle of the goddamn night again? NO! We're not a family. We never were. We're not about to be one now."

She threw up her hands. "I don't believe you — your own father. What kind of man are you to let your father go like this? What kind of family are you?"

"Where is he?" I demanded. I gave Jack my most withering look. "You don't even know."

He picked up one of his chairs and hurled it across the room. It broke against the fireplace with a terrific splintering crash, and the spokes of its back scattered like pickup sticks on the concrete floor.

Silvia looked shocked, trying to take in this side of him. I watched her face, the anger coming into it as she tried to fit this in with what she knew and loved about him. And it snagged — I could feel it — against that love and her capacity for forgiveness.

What a stupid, impotent gesture. Not any better than my own tearing into the wood. But worst of all was the terror of being in the midst of a real argument. My father and mother had never had one, at least not that I had heard. How did anyone get through it? I thought surely anger could easily last forever, that the delicate concentric circles we had carved out as orbits had just been shattered the way a hand, striking water, breaks a clear reflection into a thousand pieces.

"You didn't tell your sister? Why — you're afraid for her? She's the one that got the *huevos* in your family," Silvia shouted.

Whatever the word meant, he understood it, and it was the worst word, or the best one, she could have picked. "Come on," she said to me, grabbing her keys, "I'll take you."

Silvia ran back to the house. Jack sank into a chair. The only thing he could think of to do was close his eyes against us. He looked like a little boy practicing and practicing that protection until it was impenetrable and complete.

I'd assumed all along my father had gone back to New Orleans, that he was sitting there writing poems — sestinas or villanelles — in some crumbling garret in the French Quarter. The thought that he was anywhere near us was eerie, even disturbing. And if Jack was refusing him entrance to his house . . . had he even asked? I wasn't sure I wanted to go with her, but things were set in motion now, and there seemed no other choice but to take it all the way to its conclusion.

I left Jack sitting there. His elbows on his knees, he put

his head into his hands. I wanted to stop, to sit down next to him, talk it out, but I was moving in a stupor, as if I'd been thoroughly hypnotized and could be directed anywhere by whoever had the stronger voice.

The St. Francis Kitchen and Shelter was an abandoned warehouse in the barrio of South Tucson wedged in between the Salazar and Sons Emporium and a tortilla factory. Men stood in a narrow strip of shade that was shrinking fast as the sun went higher over the building. They carried bedrolls and plastic bags; their clothes were stiff with dirt and sweat. Some were Indians, some Mexican, some just plain white, but all were an almost equal brown from being so long in the sun. There was not a single woman among them. A black-sleeved hand pushed open the front door and they filed in slowly, something almost sweet and polite in their pace.

Silvia and I sat across the street in her truck, the engine off, watching.

"I'll go in with you."

I shook my head, no.

"I'll wait for you then — I'll be right here."

I swung my legs out of the truck and stood up in the hot, tarry street. He had called from here, from a pay phone, Silvia had said. I walked through the open door into a large, bare room lined with rows of tables like we used to eat off of in the cafeteria at school. The tables were low — built for children — and the men looked huge as they hunched over their bowls. I scanned the dozen or so sitting down, the few left in line by the steam table. He wasn't there. But all of them turned to stare at me as I came into the room. I stood in front of them and showed them a snapshot of my father — the most recent one I had — of him sitting in his office, looking up from his Hermes typewriter, his glasses sliding down his nose, not looking particularly pleased to be caught off guard. I held it up in front of me, as if I were giving a book report in school.

"Has anybody seen this man?"

They looked dutifully at the picture. A boy spoke. He was not any older than I was.

"Yeah. I saw him."

"Where?"

The boy shrugged. His brown hair looked sun-bleached, despite its oiliness. He was so deeply tanned he looked as if he'd never spent a day of his life indoors.

"I only saw him once," he added. "A big guy. Didn't look like he'd been on the road long — too neat."

"How long ago?" My heart was banging against the wall of my chest.

He thought hard, looked around as if somebody else could give him the answer, but no one else seemed to want to help.

"Maybe a week ago. Maybe less," he continued. "He was selling newspapers on a corner on Congress Street to get gas money."

Too late. I knew it.

"Did you see him after that?"

"Once, maybe twice."

"Are you sure?"

He looked suddenly guarded.

"Look, I'm not the law — I'm his daughter."

They all stared at me then, as if they couldn't imagine a daughter coming after one of them.

"Give it up," one of them said. Nobody else said a word.

I walked over to the steam table. A man in a clerical collar pushed open a swinging door from the kitchen, lugging a kettle of soup so full I was afraid it would spill and burn him. He set the pot down and wiped his hands on a white apron.

"Please, help yourself," he said gently.

I took a bowl of soup. I wasn't in the least bit hungry, but his offer made me want to accept something from him. I walked over to an empty table and sat down. I just wanted to sit there for a minute in the last place he'd been. I tried to feel his freedom. Was this what he wanted? I watched the reflection of the ceiling fan reduced to the size of a pinwheel whirling crazily inside the spoon I held in my hand.

The boy came to my table, dropped a napkin by my bowl.

"I drew you a map," he said, as I unfolded it. "There's a place some of us hole up in to sleep when the sermons in this place get to be too much." He left me sitting there.

Now that I had the map, I knew I had to follow it. But what was there to say? None of us were going to change our minds, nobody was going to be convinced to go back home — there wasn't a home to go to.

Silvia read everything she needed to know on my face. But still she asked, "Was he there?"

I shook my head — both yes and no.

"Do you want to talk?" she asked.

I shook my head again.

"*Mija,*" she said, and touched my hand. I just stared at her hand, so small against my own.

She started up the truck. In the side-view mirror I saw a man pushing a heavy cart up the street. A row of small silver bells rang with the motion of the wheels. He was bent forward, the cart heavy with ice — popsicles in all colors of the rainbow. He stopped by our truck window. "*Paletas?*" he asked. "*Muy dulce y frio,*" he added hopefully.

"*Gracias, no. Lo siento, lo siento mucho,*" Silvia said, leaning across me. He shrugged and smiled and pushed on. Out of the side mirror I saw doors open on the long barrio houses, and children dashed into the street to follow him.

We drove back to Oracle in silence, but the roar of the air conditioner as it dabbed at the 110-degree heat filled in the void. She asked me once more if I wanted to talk, but I couldn't even open my mouth.

I swear Jack hadn't moved from the chair the whole time I'd been gone. I kept going until I reached the kitchen. I sat down on the floor, not quite trusting my balance, and leaned my back against the refrigerator with my legs splayed out in front of me. The terra cotta tiles felt cool on the backs of my legs. Silence from the other room. The refrigerator rumbled behind me, sending a steady vibration into my back. The lights flickered, pulsed above. The thermostat shut off the compressor. A thudding silence. I heard feet in cowboy boots. Jack. They stopped by the kitchen counter. The boots pivoted on the heavy heels, the toes pointed toward me. Came to me. He squatted down — I could hear his knees crack as he did. He shifted, then sat down next to me, his legs outstretched. As long as mine. As long as mine. I heard Silvia's quick little steps down the hall and the sound of the screen door as she let herself out.

I listened to the small bodies of insects hurtle into the screen, the gauzy barrier between them and the world inside.

I looked at him, his arms hugging his knees, containing himself, one eye speaking to me, the other looking over my shoulder. He looked *little*. It seemed to me in that moment that if we'd grown up together it would have been me fighting on the playground with any kids who called him names. I would have been his only best friend.

"Why wouldn't you come with me?" I asked without looking at him.

He sighed with a weariness that surprised me. You'd think he'd been asked this a hundred times, or maybe he'd tried to answer it inside himself just as often. "I didn't want to see him. He most certainly doesn't want to see us."

"How do *you* know what he wants? Why would he come here if he didn't expect to see us?"

"Believe me — I *do* know. He's finally living the life he's wanted to live all along. He can keep moving, away from everything that haunts him. If he thinks he's going to get our blessing," Jack balled up his fist, "he's fucking mistaken."

"Who haunts him?" I asked, smirking. "Zeus? My mother? You and me?"

"Clara's enough."

I racked my brain, but the name didn't register right away. He studied me, and when I met his gaze I saw something close to pity in his eyes. "You don't know anything, do

you?" There was no meanness in his voice, just an over-
whelming tiredness, and an expression of utter dread on his
face as if he were being forced into something he could no
longer avoid. He reached into his back pocket for his wallet,
unfolded the thin leather envelope that had taken on the
curve of his hip. The picture on his driver's license stared
through the scratched plastic window. It didn't even look
like him — it had been taken before the beard. He reached
behind the license and pulled out a cracked sepia oval print
and held it out to me. Two children — the girl, seven or
eight years old, had her arms around an older, dark-haired
boy. "He gave this to me. That's him when he was ten. And
that's his sister, Clara." Clara was only a name on a headstone to me, marking the grave my father visited every
year, the one I kept visiting after he stopped, as if she might
feel lonely without that annual homage, those birthday
flowers laid beneath the stone with her name and the dates
that marked her brief life. I bent down to see her closer. "I
heard all about *that*," I said. Tell me something I don't
know, I thought. In the photograph they were sitting on a
porch step. Their clothes were light — muslin — the way
the clothes of summer always are. It could have been me
and Jack — the resemblance was that striking, the age dif-
ference that close. She must have gotten typhoid fever soon
after that — that's what my father said she died of — but at
the time the picture was taken she didn't look sick at all.

"He shot her. His own sister. She was four years old."
Jack's voice was flat, completely devoid of inflection or feeling. "An accident — his father's gun."

My mind lurched backward, careening through all my

memories, trying to pick up the clues. The way he had
stood at that headstone to leave the bruised wildflowers
he'd held too tightly on the walk to the graveyard. The way
he'd always come home afterward, emptied. The way he
walked through the world as if he were being shadowed —
Clara's shadow pursuing him from behind, my mother's
shadow leading him on. The gods choreographing the
black-sheep steps of his life.

I was afraid to look at Jack, but I made myself do it,
needing to see if his eyes reflected the coldness of his voice
or if they had a different story to tell. He looked as impenetrable as the ironwood he worked with.

"He thought everything he loved just disappeared," Jack
said, his fingers flicking at the dark like those of a magician
who's just produced a dove out of thin air. "If it hadn't
already, it would, soon enough," he added. He cracked his
knuckles, one at a time, something I'd never noticed that he
did. He finished one entire hand before he spoke again. "I
didn't know anything about it until I came to Virginia.
That's what he told me. That night when I got there. He
said if he didn't go, something else would happen to you.
That's what I was supposed to tell you. He couldn't do it."
He rested his hands on his thighs. "So now I've told you,"
he said wearily. "The last of the secrets."

"That's no secret," I said, acting as if I had known all
along about Clara, about why my father needed to leave.
Something twisted and broke loose inside me. My inner
workings, a mainspring, snapped. My own secret, loose
now, coming to light.

I took the napkin out of my jeans pocket, unfolded it

and laid it on the floor between us as if it were the high card that would end the game. I smoothed it with my hand.

"There's one more secret. You can come with me, or not, but I'm going," I said.

Sunset had finished an hour ago, but the light hung on as if the land were so saturated all day long by light that it exuded from the earth long after the source disappeared. On the straightaway, the narrow road shone silver from the moon behind us. We were our father's children. We needed the highway, the small, anonymous space of a moving vehicle to get to the heart of the matter. The image of him with Clara was inside both of us now — the first thing we had together that explained something of our lives.

His concentration freed from · steering and shifting down, Jack began to tell me what he'd been saving up. There was, it seemed, always one more story to tell, one more secret in front of mine. I leaned back in the seat and let it come, and he told it as if it were a story he knew by heart. Part of me wished some things would stay hidden, but I was hungry for every word. At first I thought the story was going to be about someone else, one more family member hiding in the wings, but it was about himself.

"You once asked me if my father ever came to visit after he left. Sure, I'd gone to visit *him*, but we never did anything together, just the two of us. It was always the four of us, you and your mother, once a year on your birthday." He tapped his fingers incessantly on the steering wheel. It soon got on my nerves. "Usually I'd take the train — we lived in Boston then and you were in Great Barrington. But once he

called my mom to say he would be in town and wanted to
take me to the circus. I was eleven then. My mother bun-
dled me up, gave me her Brownie camera to use, made me
wait on the porch for him. She didn't even want to see him.
I guess she decided I needed a man's influence, but probably she only hoped he'd give me some money — he'd never
sent any. We couldn't even afford a TV.

"So, he pulls up in this huge gray Hudson I'd never
seen."

"He wrecked it, or maybe he just ran it into the ground.
We didn't have it long," I said.

Jack looked annoyed that I'd interrupted, that I even had
knowledge of any of the details that belonged to him.

"He asked me how I'd been, as if it had only been a
week since he'd seen me instead of a year. Fine, I told him.

"He drove two blocks to a drugstore, where you stood
on the curb waiting with your mother. I couldn't believe it.
I thought this was my day with him alone. Why did everything have to include you?" I stole a glance at him. His face
a mask of barely controlled pain, he slammed the gearshift
from third to second as we crested the pass in the Tucson
Mountains. I hardly dared breathe.

"Right away you put the armrest down between us. You
rested your arm there and said, 'You can put your arm here,
too, if you want.'" His imitation of my five-year-old voice
was ludicrous, insulting, like that of a boy in the third grade
mercilessly teasing a girl on the playground. "You'd left
room for me. I guess I hesitated too long because you took
my arm and set it on the armrest. You said, 'We're going to
ride the elephants when we get there.' I don't remember

what I said. I just remember feeling mad. I stared straight into the back of my father's head. Your mother slid right over next to him. You imitated your mother — you leaned against me, and the four of us drove around like two couples on some kind of double date. *Jesus.*" He drove down the other side of the pass way too fast. I held on to the handle above the glove box, gripped it tightly. I was afraid he wasn't paying attention to the road, that he was so caught up in the story we'd career off the edge. There was no guardrail and the drop-off was hundreds of feet down to the desert floor. Maybe he wanted to kill us both. What little knowledge I had of him *was* a dangerous thing. I had no idea how far his anger would go, whether he was capable of harm.

"You did ride the elephant that day. We stood in line and you could hardly wait your turn. All I remember was I didn't want to go — I thought I was either too big for that, or too small — all I wanted to do was sit with my father, but he was with your mother. Her arm was always tucked through his. It seemed she never let go."

I watched Jack's face in the faint light from the speedometer and gauges. I remembered the first time he told me this story at the swap meet when he won the prize and I picked the toy elephant. That time when he told it he'd laughed as if he were telling the story of a cute, tough, little kid. This time, it was different. This time it had teeth. I leaned back against the seat, bracing myself. He steered wildly, the tires screamed.

"You raced right up to that goddamn elephant and climbed on, and I was too scared to get up behind you. Or maybe I just didn't fucking want to because *he* wanted us up there together. Then the bastard had the nerve to make me take your picture!" He glared at me as if I were making him tell this story, as if it served me right. "I *pretended* to. And the stupid thing is, I can't get it out of my head."

The way he held the wheel, the way his whole body leaned into the curves, was exactly like the way my father drove. I reached over and jerked the steering wheel hard. I didn't care what happened, I just wanted him to stop before the story poisoned me too. The truck swerved in a crazy snake shape on the road. I thought we were going to turn over. For a second I hoped we would, that we would be hurt but alive, and afterward we could be grateful and forgiving. But the gods had other, more subtle things in mind. We slid harmlessly into soft sand at the shoulder and jerked to a stop.

The engine shuddered and died. He leaned forward. I thought he was going to start the truck, but he only rested against the steering wheel, looking out at the stars — one of them had just fallen, streaked straight down from the sky. "I couldn't keep him from going," he said. His voice broke, but he reined it back in.

"Neither could I."

We sat there in the dark, looking through the windshield at the stars, at the ones that fell with a frequency that astonished me. It seemed the whole universe was breaking apart, spilling down. The idea was there, wedged between us, along with the map on the seat. We didn't have to go. We could turn back. We could let it be. No one would be the wiser, or any sadder. But we were so close. We were like orphans I'd read about, who spent years tracking down their parents but chickened out at the last second, couldn't bring themselves to knock on the door, afraid, after all that anticipation, that the real picture was never, ever going be the way you saw it in your mind.

He tried to start the truck but had difficulty doing it. The battery was weak. For a second it seemed the truck had made the decision for us. But the engine caught. We were going.

It was uncanny just how close we were. We didn't drive more than a mile from where I'd forced us off the road. Jack parked the truck at a pullout. He told me to stay close, that the path was hard to see. I followed his white shirt through the dark.

A skeleton of an enormous house made out of field-stone, thick as a fortress, loomed out of nowhere, its four walls and glassless windows, its empty doorway — all of it standing wide open, the roof burned off, the inner walls destroyed. Gutted clean by fire, the rock walls seemed strengthened by its ordeal.

"Welcome to Camelot," Jack said.

I could see the remains of a charred fireplace in what once must have been the living room, but there was no evidence of a recent fire in it. "He's not here."

"He will be — sometime tonight. His stuff's over there," he said, pointing to the farthest corner. I recognized the green duffel bag, half hidden under a tarp, the duct tape over a torn seam on the side.

"You know what's really weird — I used to come out here in high school with my friends — we'd drink ourselves

sick right here, break the beer bottles in that fireplace. I
used to love that sound."

I stood in the doorway, my hands braced against the
sides. I tried to imagine my father sleeping on the fieldstone
floor where his son once broke glass with a drunken anger
that probably had everything to do with him.

We both heard footsteps at the same time coming slowly up the path. Jack leapt out the window; sheer panic made
me follow. We hid like two kids in danger of being caught
playing with fire. We inched our way back into a position
where we could look in without being seen.

We watched our father step through the doorway, a
plastic jug of water in his hand. Our hearts were pounding
so loud I thought the double beat must surely be audible.
He looked carefully around, listening. Surely he must sense
his own children there, instinctively, the way an animal can
pick up the scent of its own kind on the wind.

I felt that if I watched him in secret for a while I might
understand something new about him. But he just set
down the water and pulled some firewood from the corner.
He knelt before the fireplace to lay the fire, picked up a
pack of matches from the broken mantelpiece. The dry
mesquite lit easily and soon grew to a steady flame. He
poured some of the water into a mess-kit pot with a handle,
laid a grate that looked like a rack from an oven over the
fire, and set the pot of water to boil. He dropped a tea bag
into a Circle K commuter mug and sat down to wait. It
amazed me to see him still doing something I'd seen him
do every night of my life. I even knew what kind of tea it
was — Twining's Irish Breakfast.

I felt Jack shift his weight. I turned my head to look at him. Our faces were inches apart. I looked straight into his eyes and saw they were my father's eyes for sure — guarded and wounded. And his mouth — his hard, thin-lipped mouth was beginning to tremble. All desire to kiss him was gone; what remained was a more oblique gesture. I leaned lightly against him, rested my forehead against his. He did not pull away. I thought if I tried hard enough I could hear him thinking.

Through the open windows and doors, up through the burned-away roof, came the sound of our father singing. I felt Jack's thought as my own reached him — neither of us had ever heard him sing. He wasn't half bad, either. It was not a happy song; neither was it particularly sad. I'd like to think it was a kind of calling, the way Orpheus sang to Eurydice to bring her back, but it was probably something by Cole Porter, whom he'd listened to for years.

There he was, at home in the world without us, in a house that looked as if it had been in the blitz. There he was, singing, in spite of everything.

I pulled away from Jack. I got to my feet, but immediately he yanked me back down.

"You're not going in there," he hissed.

"I am so," I hissed back, but I wasn't really sure. Jack looked at me in pity — or was it envy? I hoisted myself through the window, then lost my balance as I crouched on the sill. I fell headfirst into the room.

My father lurched to his feet and backed away, staring, his eyes searching the dark.

I was on my hands and knees, my hair thrown forward.

I started to lift my head slowly, by degrees, felt my hair spilling soundlessly back into place.

"Auralee?" he said, his voice hoarse, incredulous.

I jerked my head up all the way then rocked back to my heels. My hands flew over my mouth, just soon enough to stop the cry that wanted to come out.

I stayed on my knees, waiting for him to recognize me. How could he not be disappointed when he realized it was not my mother come to find him?

His face began so many different expressions but finished none. It darkened with fear, then cleared with the start of a smile, then went blank. He held his arms out, but not to me — it was a gesture of helplessness, a kind of surrender. I wanted to back out of the room. I wanted to not have shown myself at all, to stay hidden with Jack, watching our father through a window — a man who finally becomes himself because he believes there is no one there to see him.

"I'm sorry," I said. Such little words covering huge regrets, not the least of which was that I had found him.

Firelight raked the stone walls and the broken mantelpiece above the cave of the fireplace. The stars wheeled across the open roof. A plane passed over, descending slowly toward the airport a few miles away. I could almost feel the gods gathering above us to watch, hesitantly I thought, as if maybe they'd pushed us all too far this time.

I got myself to my feet, swaying slightly before I found my balance. I was, in some fleeting way, like a parent, frustrated with love for a runaway child, as he had once been with me, unsure of what feeling to put forth first — relief or reprimand?

There was no time left and way too much to talk about. "Why did you leave?" is all I managed to say.

"Why?" He looked out the window, as if something out there could help him, an understudy, or the Greek chorus whispering his next line. He came up, not with an answer, but a question I was equally unprepared for. "Why did *you?*"

I ran through the whole rationale in two seconds of why to keep quiet — some things are better left unsaid, what you don't know won't hurt you, ignorance is bliss, white lies are acts of kindness, etc., etc., etc. But I was never going to be this close to telling him again. "To have a grand adventure, like you." I waved my hands in the air, spread them wide to indicate the magnitude of what I'd had in mind. "Except mine," I said, dropping my hands, "was a complete disaster . . ."

"The gods," he broke in, "they don't let you get away with anything."

My voice rose, and I gave up trying to stop it. "I don't want to hear that crap about the gods. I want you to hear what *I* have to say."

He closed his eyes. Minutes seemed to pass, but I'm sure it was only seconds. When he opened them I was almost certain they were filling with tears. "I think," he said so softly I had to move closer to hear, "I think I can't stop anything from breaking. I think some things broke because of me. I tried to leave before anything could happen to you."

"Too late."

This version of the truth was more terrible. I wanted to push it back, let him be innocent, let myself be unscathed, let the gods shoulder the blame that was surely theirs.

"But you're not going to break," he said. He studied my face, and I had the feeling I was slowly coming into focus. "No," he said. "You won't break. Not you. Jack, maybe, but not you."

I stood before my father, torn between pride and despair. I was thrilled he thought of me as strong, but I felt almost physically sick, too, that in so many ways I had misrepresented myself and so would not ever be able to break down. I was my father's daughter, which I now understood to mean that I was bound by an unspoken, greater need to protect him.

The truth was all over the place, sifting down, like pieces of stars from broken, dying galaxies. He was traveling light. He could take one more thing. "You're wrong," I said. "I already broke. You just didn't see."

I no longer felt that I had a body, that I displaced even the air around me. My teeth would not even leave a mark on his skin. I searched for the one right thing to say, but it was as if language had dissolved, stranding me in a sea of vowels with no consonants left to hold the words together.

"I left before, and now I have to do it all over again, in front of you," he said. It could just as well have been what I had meant to say.

"What else, Matty? What can I do?"

"*You're* asking *me?*" I knew he meant it in a rhetorical way, but I had an answer. "You can kiss me good-bye — at least that." My voice betrayed me, and broke as I said it; it did not sound like the demand I meant it to be.

He leaned close. I felt his breath, warm against my cheek, then the kiss like a seal upon my skin. My arms were at my sides, and I felt the way I did that night wrapped in the blanket at the bottom of the stairs, the night when Jack held me and I could not hold him back. But I lifted my arms, put them around my father, and I felt so clearly then what I had only guessed at before, that even though we were within reach, we had always been beyond each other, that the distance between us was the exact calibration of our fear. We practiced leaving each other with an animal instinct for survival, which moved us out of the den farther and farther afield until one day we just kept going because what we needed was no longer in the cave of home but out there somewhere on the wind. But neither of us really left — we were always circling back, sooner or later.

I took the kiss. It wasn't enough. I felt like a person who had used up her last wish on something foolish when I could have asked for the moon. But my father didn't have the moon, just a few faint stars whose light had lasted beyond their lives, gone but shining anyway.

"Jack's here too, isn't he?" He looked toward the window as if he knew exactly where his son was hiding. He waited. I waited. I could feel Jack listening, waiting too. Nobody moved. Nobody could. "He's not as brave as you. You get that from your mother, not me."

I knew what Jack was doing. Nothing. But it was as if I dreamed his revenge for him. I felt his hand reach for a gun,

felt the cool metal heavy in his palm as if it were my own
hand. I knew none of these things for certain, but I was in
awe of these details, as if their appearance in my mind's eye,
in the very physical register of my body were indisputable
truths, all the verification I needed that the inevitable was
about to happen. But the thought struck me as surely as if a
shot had literally been fired, that I had no idea who he
would be aiming for. My father was turning now, walking
away, and would soon be out of range. I could not move an
inch. My father was out the door, taking leave, walking
back along the same path that Jack and I had taken to him.
He was a small, receding figure against the unlimited sky.
He'd shed the house, the car, and, I realize now, even my
mother. He looked as if he were walking toward a world
that might hold him, where the blame might finally drop
away. Or maybe this was the parting shot I had to have. I
could make it anything I wanted — it was a matter of
changing the scale. He might just as easily be a man about
to be swallowed up whole by the sky.

I felt the trembling begin in Jack's shoulder and ripple
down the length of my arm. I braced myself for the shot,
but what came was not the burning velocity of a bullet but
a terrible silence.

I made myself move toward the window. My father was
gone, a speck moving away along the path. Terrified, I
leaned over the sill. Jack was sitting on the ground, his arms
around his knees, rocking back and forth. There was no
gun, not that I could see. He looked up at me, his face utterly blank.

I pushed my hand through the glassless window, held out my hand to him. I could feel him wanting, not wanting, to take it, knowing in my heart of hearts he could not. My brother stood. Then he jumped up, his hands catching the ledge, and pulled himself up by his own two hands like a swimmer from a pool.

We walked through the house together, then headed back down the path. Planes flew over every ten minutes. After a while I lost track of how many. Planes full of people, some coming home, some arriving for the first time. I walked with the weight of what I knew, a burden of knowledge, an Eve on her way out of the too-good-to-be-true garden, into the lackluster, barely livable world.

My last week in Arizona with Jack, the desert pulled me with the same seduction that my father's old journeys pulled me out of my bedroom window in Virginia. My father was on his way to New Orleans, and Silvia started packing her bags to move in with Jack. What I wanted more than anything was to disappear.

I thought of what Ben had once told me about what happened before a seizure, and that's where I wanted to go — and stay: that hallowed world where light revealed each thing it touched, where time was lulled, slowed at last to the pace of graceful things. I was suddenly afraid of how much I missed him.

I took Silvia's Toyota only because she'd left her keys in it. Jack never let his keys out of sight. I released the brake and rolled silently down the hill, jump-starting it as I hit the main road. I headed west, toward California where the sun had gone, but then I saw a sign for a town with the improbable name of Why, and I knew it was the perfect place to go. Five miles from Why I changed my mind, took a dirt track and headed south, toward Mexico.

I ran out of road after nearly an hour of bumping on a washed-out path. The terrain was too rocky to drive over, especially without four-wheel drive. I got out and walked. I was in the grip of the gods now. I no longer had to think.

I counted steps until I was out of numbers, until my brain finally shut up and I became a shape simply moving toward a range of mountains that walked on their own, teasing me, maintaining the same distance between us. The full moon was bright as shaded sun. My shadow leaked out of my shoes, spreading before me, slightly out of sync with my movements as if trying to wrench itself from the place at my feet where it was bound.

I stopped abruptly; exhaustion took over. My body ached. I became an ancient version of myself in minutes while my mind reeled backward to a single idea, away from all the complications of desire. The hunger at the bottom of hunger. Touch before the hand. Real thirst.

I came at last to the image of my father, which I'd been following all along. He was alone, and what he headed toward was not the mirage my mother would have made in that shimmering climate, but an unpeopled horizon. He left a single set of tracks on the ground with his own two feet. He was happy there, without guilt or want. He'd set a suitcase down at the desert's edge, and already the wind had opened it. Spilling out of the leather box, my mother's robe, a book of poems by Keats, a schedule of trains. My mother entered my peripheral vision, beckoning, no longer to him, but to me. All I wanted now was to be homing toward her, imprinted like a fledgling bird whose survival depended on following the first thing seen at birth, always, always keeping her in sight.

I heard it. Not wings, not her, but the cascading scree from a hill behind her. Not wings, but a man, his arms weighted heavily, swinging, ponderous. The sound of contained water. A single bright eye, roving side to side, its light sweeping the world. He didn't see me — I was beyond that now. I could walk right up to him, pass through him. He'll swear it was only the wind briefly turning warm.

I stood up, the eye of light catching my face as I rose into it. He yelled and dropped the water.

I was disappointed to still be so visible, to feel what I assumed was my weightless soul come slamming back into my body, which, to my surprise, took it back gladly.

He stared at me. Both of us were blue in the moonlight. Blue people in the middle of nowhere. Maybe it was the plastic jugs of water, tacky reminders of the eternal presence of commerce, that brought the real world back. He seemed vulnerable, shackled by thirst. He was no god, only a man. He was older than Jack, younger than my father. A ring gleamed from his left hand. He said something in Spanish which I didn't understand, but his voice was soft, kind. I was not afraid.

He held one of the jugs of water toward me. I took it

and drank deeply, greedily; water dripped down my chin. It was warm and tasted of dust and plastic and captured sunlight.

He must have thought I was lost, or insane. I had heard about illegal aliens from Mexico trying to get across the border into the States, sometimes dying of thirst because the journey was longer than they'd realized. He was probably risking his life to sneak into my country, while I must have looked like somebody who had stumbled right into the thick of it with no water, with no knowledge of the desert or respect for its dangers.

He picked up his jugs of water and started walking again. He stopped, looked back at me, waiting. My body moved without thought. I followed. Maybe that's all I'd come for — someone to point me in a particular direction.

There was only the sloshing sound in the half-empty jugs of water, our footsteps, and the high squeak of bats darting between saguaros, feeding on the new fruit, pollinating the last flowers. Every once in a while the man would stop dead in his tracks and just listen. Then, satisfied with the silence, he would move on. I was so tired I could barely move, and every time I fell behind he waited patiently for me to catch up.

There was a kind of reassuring rhythm to all this, an endurance test that I knew I would not fail. I was a body now, joints working, tendons flexing, muscles contracting, expanding. A body simply covering ground, without thinking, all feeling pushed outward from the heart, distributed equally, limb to limb.

My life was a relay, and somehow I had been passed to

this person to whom I could not speak but with whom I shared the common language of covering ground. It hadn't been a straight line — if anything, it was a kind of circle, closing in on the idea of reunion. My mother, my father, and even Jack would step out from behind the curtain and reveal themselves when I had finally passed some test whose rules were always unwritten, always changing.

We stopped for more water. It was almost gone. The moon was partly hidden by a hill. We stood near its flank, drinking the tepid water. As I tilted my head back for the last of it, an enormous black bird rose straight up from behind the hill, beating its wings with a deafening roar. The man dropped the jugs and ran for cover. The light of the bird blinded us, its wings beat so furiously the sand rose around us and the empty jugs bounced and cartwheeled away. The bird came for me. Its beating wings whipped my hair around me. I covered my ears and crouched low.

How easy it was to cross a line — the post office steps, the border between one country and another, one race and another, between the living and the dead. The man — he was running for the edge of the circle of light into the safety of darkness, but each time he'd get there the edge of light would move. He darted like a jackrabbit beneath a plummeting owl, pushing against the membrane of light that held him while I watched, helpless, yet exempt from what pursued him. The light moved across the desert. I saw his shape stoop and pick up something, then straighten up, brandishing it. He fell. I ran toward him. He lay face down, his arms out. Then he raised his head. He was not hurt, but had simply thrown himself to the ground like any soldier facing fire, forced into surrender. And even though part of me was starting to realize they had only fired blanks to stop him, I was terrified — I might be out of my mind, but at least I was in my own country — that somehow I had betrayed him, that I had slowed him down. If he hadn't waited for me, he might be home free.

I barely remember the ride to the Border Patrol station at Lukeville. Jack and Silvia came for me late that afternoon. I first heard Silvia's voice, angry, on the other side of a wall.

They both looked anxious as I walked into the waiting room. For a moment I understood something about my father — that inability to explain what must appear to be crazy behavior. I ached with one clear thought, that I had been stripped clean of everything and I felt so light I thought the air could lift me. I had no explanation. I didn't need or want one now. I just let them take me back to Tucson.

On the way to the parking lot, I saw the man, alone in a green school bus that was headed toward the highway. It turned left, south. I wondered how long it would be before he was ready to try again, if he would make it next time. This is what I've come to think, that I betrayed that man by slowing him down, harmed him the way my father harmed people — without actually meaning to, but inflicting damage that lingers throughout a life just the same.

Jack and Silvia did everything they could to take care of me. At least they fed me and tried to talk to me, but part of me was still wandering in the desert south of Why. I went through the motions, I tried to return to the living, I put one foot in front of the other, but when I looked at my feet they seemed to be someone else's. They were attached to me but without feeling or directed motion. I didn't feel I had the will to hold anyone's attention — the living or the disappeared. So I packed my bags for California — went through with that lie of a story. I think Jack, especially, was relieved. His house was not my home — it was Silvia's now, as it should be. Of course, there was an open invitation. "Come back, anytime." Of course, I never did. Jack sold the house the following year, and they both moved to Guadalajara — she'd inherited her father's estate — and the two of them made their own family there.

The day I left Arizona, Jack took me to the Greyhound station. I'd come full circle, so to speak. I was back on the bus, back on a road to somewhere. When he pulled me close to say good-bye his arms held me so tightly I thought my ribs would crack. I didn't have any tears left. It seemed for a second that Jack was going to cry, but if he did, I never saw it. He turned away. "Keep in touch," he called over his shoulder as I climbed aboard the bus.

Hours later I crossed the line into California. I was sure the "Welcome" sign had not been put up for me.

louds again. No rain. Even the desert is running on empty now. The cactus, which have enormous capacity for storing water, look shrunken, as if they've almost used it up. I have never felt more desolate in my life. I am running out of memories. There's nowhere left to go. A void opens up behind me and I'm plummeting now, as if I've fallen backward off a bridge and the water, rather than getting closer, only moves farther away.

There's nothing left to photograph. As a joke, I take a picture of my bare foot.

It absolutely infuriates me that Carrie Silver hasn't left anything worth snooping for. There's a locked drawer in her desk that's been bugging me ever since I got here, and today it calls to me — I force it open with a kitchen knife. Nothing at all in there except the deed to the house, a birth cer-tificate, the title to her car. Why she needs to hide that I don't know — she left her car with someone else. The woman doesn't trust me, obviously. Maybe on the phone I sounded like someone who would rummage through her things. So I go ahead and rummage some more through the papers, and I find, wedged against the back of the drawer, a perfect symbol to mock me, as if she'd planted it there. A Mexican Día de los Muertos, Day of the Dead, figurine, no more than three inches tall — a skeleton with a crazy, leering grin on its skull. I slam the drawer shut.

Silvia once told me the dead need comforting just like anyone else, that they still want their favorite foods brought to their graves on that day once a year. Before I left Arizona, she took me to Hermosillo to visit her grand-mother's grave. She put a can of Pepsi and a plate of ginger cookies made in the shape of pigs on the freshly swept dirt. Maybe Mexico could have a sense of humor about death, but I didn't know what to make of the casualness of the rit-ual. Death, in the Grover family, was serious, secret busi-ness. Silvia gave me a sugar skull to eat, and I bit down hesitantly on the white, crunchy cranium. It was sweeter than I imagined.

At least I heard directly that my father was dying, didn't have to learn about it thirdhand through some stranger, the way I'd learned nearly everything else about my family.

Seven years ago Jack called to tell me. His voice was scratchy through the wires stretched across the border from Mexico. A bad connection, but still he managed to reach me in San Francisco.

"Dad's in Virginia, Matty. In Rappahannock. He's had a stroke. He's dying."

All the way to Virginia — on a plane this time because I needed the speed — I kept thinking, why was it Jack that the hospital tracked down — why not me? But I knew the answer. He was easy to find. He'd been living in one house in Guadalajara. I'd moved twelve times in the same four years. And my father — all that intrepid traveling, fancy-free, and now he'd gone home to die, within shouting distance, practically, from the very place he was born. He had only taken me to that town once, "a place," he'd said, "where dreams belong to the devil." The place looked so dull I couldn't imagine the devil even passing through. My father had driven me past the house where he was born — he was born right in his mother's bed — but the house looked small, gray, disappointingly ordinary.

I went to the hospital where Jack said our father had been admitted. I'd never set foot in a hospital before. When my mother had checked into one I wasn't allowed inside. She'd never walked out of the hospital again. This hospital loomed large. Its halls swallowed me down, down, down to a numbered room. I pushed open the door. Nothing in my life had prepared me for what was there. I focused on Jack first because I couldn't look at what was on the bed. He looked so much older, his beard shot through with gray, his body a little heavier, as if he and not Silvia had given birth to two children. He took my hand and pulled me gently to the foot of the bed as if I were a reluctant bride shying away from the altar. There we stood, finally, at the feet of our father.

He filled the narrow bed. He looked ancient, tired. His skin almost transparent. His mouth open, his last breath come and gone.

"You almost made it," Jack said. "Twenty minutes — that's how close you were."

I would have laughed if I hadn't been so completely stunned. We were light years away from each other, my father and I. The clock had stopped, that's all.

Jack started to leave the room. "Tell him whatever you need to," he said. "I've said what I wanted. It didn't take long." The door clicked behind him.

My hands gripped the iron bed frame. I couldn't stop staring at my father. He looked as bald and helpless as a newborn bird, mouth open, as if he only wanted to be fed.

Everyone else in the family had had their secrets forced from them sooner or later. Now it was my turn, my secret. And of course, with all due irony, it would be a one-sided conversation. If my father had waited another half hour we'd probably be having an argument, but at least he'd be listening. I didn't even try to begin. I just couldn't do it, not to this empty body, not in this hospital room. I left without saying good-bye — to Jack or to him.

What I saw, what I still see when I think of my father's face, that open, helpless mouth not saying anything, was that the gods themselves were finally out of words.

I walk out on my desert patio, sick and tired of thinking. I can't bear it. I won't have it. I'll simply stop thinking. I'll wait for Della. She'll have something to say. But today she doesn't come down the hill. This time I'll have to go up to her.

I put on some clothes. There's a gaunt, sun-darkened woman in the mirror staring back at me, a homunculus with eyes. When I put on my shoes, I have to think about how to tie them. I'm scared out of my wits that she died, that I'll find her lying in the driveway, half-eaten by coyotes.

I find Della on her hands and knees, in the garden, pushing tin can lids into wet mud. The sun glints off the honeycomb of mirrors, ripples concentrically as if a pebble has been dropped simultaneously into each. When she sees me, she sits back on her heels.

She isn't wearing her hat. Her face looks drawn, tight, pale despite the sun. Her hair defies the pins that try to hold it. Our eyes meet briefly, then cut away, as if we're both ashamed to be seen. But here we are. Here we are.

"You look terrible," she says.

"So do you."

I sit down next to her. She hands me a wooden spoon. I scoop up a glob of wet cement from the mixing bucket where a hose dribbles steadily to keep it soft. She dips her spoon in, then slaps the mud down. I do the same. We pat the mud with the backs of wooden spoons. She shoves a cardboard box toward me. It's full of a weird assortment of odds and ends — buttons, combs, jewelry, pocket mirrors in pink plastic frames, silver conchos, turquoise beads. We push these things, one at a time, into the soft, gray mortar. The mirrors catch the red reflection of a hummingbird's throat; the bird hovers above us for a few seconds before it zings away.

We work steadily, without speaking, stopping occasionally to drink water from a thermos. I don't ever want to get up from here. I just want to stay with her in wordless collaboration, pressing things into the ground without thinking too much about it, to be next to a woman who knows something, but not too much, about me. I think of what my mother would have been like had she lived to be so old. In my mind, she looks something like Della. And here I am, her daughter, kneeling next to her, helping her do this mindless, beautiful thing. But even though we take our time, the last of the cement dries to a gritty mush in the bottom of the bucket, and the box gives us its last offering — a cat's-eye marble. Our hands crack with dried mud.

It's Della who sees the rattlesnake first. She watches it, transfixed the way a cat is, wary, alert, calm. If she had a tail, it would twitch. The snake slides at an excruciatingly slow pace toward us and stops. I keep my eyes on Della and will myself to be like her, to slip inside her calm and stay there. The snake pauses at the edge of our creation, and to my utter amazement it drinks from the small puddle the dribbling hose continues to feed. It drinks like any other living thing, with its tongue, with a simple thirst, and somehow that makes it seem less threatening. When it has had enough, it ripples slowly through the edge of the mud, then disappears between two rocks as if pouring itself into a hole. We lean close to look at the signature it has left in the mud.

That's when I notice the trail Della herself made from the house — a series of handprints in this morning's mud, dried now — some of the prints partly erased by the legs she dragged behind.

I look at her, my face a question she can answer any way she chooses.

"I don't seem to be able to walk very well anymore," she says, her usual haughty edge gone now.

When she sees my alarm, she quickly adds, "My daughter's coming — any day now."

"*You* have a daughter?"

Della's words spill out in a steady, unstoppable stream. "I wish I didn't. She's going to swoop in here with her noisy child and a nurse to feed and wipe me." She tosses her head, indicating the statues of animals in the garden. "If I could figure out a way to do it, I'd turn *myself* to stone.

"Margaret's probably quite pleased right now." Della laughs softly. "She's always blamed me for leaving her and her father. They had to fend for themselves. She likes to remind me." Della looks up. "They were eating me alive, the two of them — that's exactly how it felt. They wanted my complete attention. Well, they didn't get it." She thrusts her chin up, her old defiance back.

Now, I see my mother checking out of her life, just as Della is doing, although my mother did this literally, as if she were checking out of a hotel. I always thought of her death at thirty-six as premature, tragic. But maybe she just had enough. I can almost see her — her firm signature on the register, the payment in cash, the final push of paper and coin and key across the counter to a poker-faced clerk. Did she get her money's worth? Did she forget anything? Would she have written my name absentmindedly on the pad of paper by the telephone? Did she know me well enough to draw me? And my father, leaving as if he were relieved at last to be driving across America alone. And me, the daughter, with all the comings and goings and my own ridiculous journey toward Jack, which I had wanted to feel was like falling in love, but was, in truth, only like falling. Now it seemed that with all these things preparing me, all I had learned was how to leave myself behind. And who, who in the world was left to come after me?

Della's voice pulls me back from Virginia, from New Jersey and New Orleans or wherever it is I've gone to. "When you first walked in here today I wanted you to leave. I'm glad you didn't because, frankly, I like your company. You don't talk too much, for one thing, and you're not a whiner — I admire that in a person. But I want the last of my peace and quiet. Alone."

"Don't ask me to go, Della, I don't want to."

"I'm not going to be around that much longer. Don't latch on to me. Give me some peace — you're the only person I can ask that of now."

I get up with some difficulty — my feet are both asleep. I can't believe she actually said that to me. I mumble something about calling me if she needs anything. I back away, waiting for the feeling to come back in my feet, but they just prickle from the straining circulation, and it's all I can do to keep from falling down.

I tell myself I'm not waiting, but I am. I'm waiting for Della to turn to me. I pace the patio, one ear tuned to the phone that must surely ring.

Mail keeps arriving for Carrie Silver, magazines mostly. I pick up an issue of *Life*. The magazine has always been a little window on the world that clearly exists elsewhere. I learned about the Summer of Love from its pictures, and I lived as if the images had been oracles, directives pulling me back and forth across the country, north and south: Woodstock, Altamont, Big Sur, L.A. But I'd made a lousy hippie. I could never "Be Here Now." I was elsewhere. Then and now.

I flip through the black and white pages and wonder about these photographers, who, in the midst of chaos, had the presence of mind to take these pictures. How did they have the time to focus, to compose, while the world was ending right in front of them? I tried to remember my own brief "combat" photography episode in Virginia, taking the picture of Jones with the police dog hanging off his arm — remembered how I'd stood there, unable to act, how Jones, always my teacher, had to tell me to press the shutter. What would I do in the middle of a war zone? Become utterly paralyzed or detached in a scary, determined way? I already knew the answer. I was the kind who became paralyzed, who hung on to hope too long and broke through windows too late.

I turn the page. The photograph there pulls me straight into its terrible, grainy center. I can't look away. It comes through my eyes and brands itself directly on the brain, where it will stay. An arrested moment — the private terror of a young girl splayed across a magazine for all the world to see. She is naked, running down a dirt road, mouth open in eternal scream. The village behind her, in flames. Her arms, outstretched, as if she has no choice left except to fly and has just realized she will never ever get off the ground. She must be nine or ten — she has no pubic hair. She is running down this road forever, sticky with the new skin of napalm, burning, burning, her home and family in ashes behind her. Her life changed forever, by a single, incendiary moment, unforgettable.

I feel her heat. I feel her coming toward the slow burn of my life. She is coming closer. She is setting fire to every-thing.

Death and burning bridges — my mother taught me the power of disappearance, what an enormous claim upon the heart it could have. She was in the hospital when I left — my father was there night and day with her. I rattled around the house, scared out of my skin, waiting for him to come home with news. Each time he came home I'd run to the door to meet him and ask, "How is she?" "Better, bet-ter" was all he'd say, but the despair on his face told me otherwise. I couldn't stand the waiting. I thought I would fly apart if I didn't *do* something, *go* somewhere.

My father had no idea how well he had prepared me for this trip. I had a map in my head, compass points clearly marked with all his old destinations. I knew which city to head for, which town came next, what state came after that. I'd been a good listener; I'd been to each place at least a dozen times in my mind. I could easily find my way there.

I didn't take anything with me except a transistor radio and the thirty-two dollars I'd saved for a guitar. I put these things in my father's small, battered, leather suitcase, which I'd taken from the hall closet the night before. The brown leather was plastered with decals: Beautiful Florida, Grand Canyon Village, Sunshine State, Visit Louisiana! When my father showed me the suitcase he said, "I've been there and back!" and I thought he probably should have painted those words right on the case — his very own slogan. The decals were living proof of his journeys. The suitcase wouldn't hold more than a spare shirt and socks, a book or two.

I pulled the small ID tag from its cracked leather holder, and it didn't come out easily, stuck to the plastic window by some Florida heat or New Orleans sticky summer night. I pulled it free, finally, and with a pen wrote over the S of his initial and made it into the M of mine.

I sat down at the desk and spread some newspaper in front of me. I held out a long hank of my hair in one hand and cut it away with a pair of paper scissors. I left it there, piled on the paper like a nest of dark brown grass. I looked at my reflection in the mirror and was shocked but pleased at how different I looked, how simple it was to change.

I left a note: "I'm not running away, exactly. I'm just going where you used to go. I'll be fine."

I left it propped up next to the hair.

I waited until it was good and dark, then I pushed the window open and lowered the suitcase by a rope into the grass below. I slid my leg over the sill, then eased the other over, grabbing for the tree where I'd propped a ladder earlier in the evening. I made my way barefoot down the rungs until my feet touched grass. I picked up the suitcase and held my shoes in my other hand, then walked.

I turned to look back at the house, the dark window where my father slept — not even realizing that I was out there, standing at the end of the yard with his suitcase in my hand, about to walk away.

The road drew an unwavering black line through fields of long grass nearly white in the moonlight. A tunnel of

trees leaned together in the slight wind. Horses, gray
shapes grazing on the hill, lifted their heads slowly as I
passed and did not stretch their long necks back to earth
until I was out of sight.

The bus depot was nothing more than a small room in the
back of the Texaco station with a bench outside. It was 2:00
A.M., and I'd walked seven miles. I hadn't counted on its
being closed. A handwritten sign on the door said to pay
the driver the fare. I waited for the bus to Baltimore, a two-
hour trip to the north.

My father had told me many times about the port of
Sparrow's Point near Dundalk just outside Baltimore. At
seventeen he had convinced the captain of a ship called the
Nora bound for Belfast that he was really twenty-one, and
he got hired as a mess boy in the galley. Each time he told it
I could feel his triumph, his passing for older than he was,
his setting out on a voyage to his ancestral home. I could
see him sneaking out to the stern as the *Nora* pulled away
to watch America rise from its shoreline, then fade away
into the curve of the earth. I liked to picture him leaning
against the railing after the night's dinner was cooked,
smoking a cigarette, and tilting his head back to see the
stars. He wouldn't have known any constellations or been
able to distinguish the steady glow of a planet from the rest,
but he would have stayed a long time in the wind and dark,
with the tent of his father's coat pulled close around him.

I didn't have to wait long. The bus came down Main Street,
its turn signal flashing orange as it swung into the station

parking lot. The door opened with a hiss, and the driver, an enormous man who seemed to spill over his seat, flicked on a small light and took out a receipt book of tickets. He wore a change maker as silver and intricate as a flute strapped onto a thick leather belt. Folds of flesh overlapped it, and he had to sit up straight to get his thumb on the levers.

"Where you goin' this time of night?" he asked.

With a tone as dead certain as I could manage, I said, "Baltimore. Give me a ticket through to Baltimore."

He looked hard at me. I stared back as if I knew where I was going, even turned the suitcase a little so he could see the stickers and held it like a shield in front of me.

"That'll be six dollars and seventy-five cents," he said, and his thumb bore down on the lever that released a quarter into his thick fingers, one of them cinched tight with a ring that would have to be cut to ever come off again.

With another hiss of escaping air the doors folded shut and sealed us in. I made my way to the back, where I could sit with my feet propped up on the wheel well. There were only three other people on the bus. They were all sleeping with their heads rolled back, mouths open. I brushed past a sailor with his white cap pulled down like a shade.

The bus ground through so many gears getting up to speed I lost track of the number. I watched the lights of town streaking back, as if the whole place were pulling away from its moorings, carried on a current out to sea. The last thing to go was the A&P parking lot where my father let me drive the car early one Sunday morning. He held on to the door handle the whole time as I slalomed around the light poles and crisscrossed the endless rows of empty parking spaces again and again, as if each pass could erase a little more of those careful white lines.

Baltimore was red with sunrise and brick row houses. Metal chairs waited on the porches, lights flashed on behind windows. It seemed strange to me, people living side by side like that, able to see inside each other's houses with a casual glance. The houses looked so old I thought they could be the very same ones my father had passed all those years ago.

It was not a clean city, and the deeper we drove into it the uglier it got. Newspapers blew across vacant lots and stuck to the chain-link fencing. When we stopped at a light I saw a man pissing against a wall, a dark pool spreading into the dust at his feet. At the next light there was a woman, her bare arms the color of piecrust dough sitting on a stoop; she was smoking a cigarette with one hand, holding on to a baby with the other. During the two long minutes from red to green, she watched the smoke drift slowly in the still air. She never once looked at the baby.

The bus lurched into the station. Everyone staggered to their feet, groping for their belongings.

The driver was writing something on a clipboard as I passed him. "Watch your step," he said without looking up. "And watch your back, too." I looked quickly behind me. He shook his head and his body jiggled as he laughed. "No, sweet thing, out there." His forefinger poked at the air and pointed to the world outside the bus. His thumb flipped the change meter four times and he took my hand and poured a stream of quarters into it. "Refund. Get yourself some breakfast. You'll be needing it."

I sat down at the counter and ordered some cornflakes that came in their own little box. A boy in a raincoat sat two stools away twirling a spoon around in an empty cup of coffee. We kept stealing glances at each other in the mirror behind the counter. I watched his reflection move toward me and sit on the stool next to me. He had dark crescent moons under his eyes. His hair was coal black, which only made his face whiter. He looked as if he hadn't slept in days, maybe all his life, but he smiled when he saw my suitcase, and his face, for a moment, was bright, awake, alive.

"You been to all those places?"

"Some."

"You don't look old enough to just be on vacation."

I shrugged. He didn't wait for an answer but went on.

"This is my third time out. They don't even try to look for me anymore."

He said his name was Luke. He said he was seventeen. "From New Hope, where there isn't any."

Maybe he was telling the truth, maybe not. But I felt as if I could call myself anything I wanted, try out a new age, be from somewhere else. So I told him my name was Luz, after a Spanish girl I liked in school who told me her name meant light. Luke didn't know any Spanish and heard the word as Luce. "Short for Lucy, right?" I didn't try to tell him any different. I also said I was seventeen and from Paris,

Virginia, which was just a place where my father and I stayed in a motel once, but a place I liked the sound of because of its exotic implications.

"You got a particular place in mind to go to?" he asked my face in the mirror.

"Sparrow's Point," I told him. "It's a port somewhere near here."

"What if I go with you?" he said.

"Why would you want to — don't you have your own place to go to?"

"I've been sitting here all night watching people, just waiting to see if somebody came through who looked like they had an idea where they were going. When I saw you and that suitcase I knew, and I said to myself, 'There she is. She's the one.' You look like you're going *toward* something."

Suddenly, I thought of my father's dire predictions of the gods and how they struck people down. I felt a little wary, as if I might possibly be setting out on one of those ill-fated journeys the Greeks were always going on. But I felt immune, too, in some strange way, because I thought the gods had tired of us and had moved on to someone else by now. They were busy enough with my mother. They didn't have time for me. In any case, I decided to take Luke along, more for company than any kind of protection — he didn't look like the kind of person who had ever been able to prevent anything from happening to him; he seemed to be tired from the effort of trying.

We looked for an information booth to see about getting another bus. For a minute I felt worried, wondering if maybe my father made this place up, just as I had picked myself another name. Maybe there was no way to follow him, maybe it was all a lie, a false trail zigzagging around a secret life.

"Dundalk bus is at Gate 6, stops at Sparrow's Point," Luke said, his finger pressing against the word halfway down the posted schedule, underlining its simple truth with his bitten nail.

Dundalk was not the misty, green place on the Irish coast for which it was named, but a smog-gray and grimy port bristling with orange cranes on the Chesapeake Bay. I felt sick with a growing disappointment I couldn't fully admit to yet. The adrenaline that kept me going all night suddenly left me feeling empty and hungry and thin. But this was just Dundalk, and I told myself Sparrow's Point would be a better place. Even its name sounded promising.

The bus continued on to a much smaller port. A single ship, unloaded, with all its water marks showing like the hem of a slip, was tethered to the pier. The bus let us out in front of a place called the Streamliner Diner that flared silver in the sun. We went in and sat down in a red vinyl booth.

"What'll you two have?" The waitress thumbed through her order pad and didn't even look at us.

"Bacon and eggs, over easy, and a side of grits with extra butter," Luke said. Then he turned to me. "You got money, don't you?"

"A little."

"Well, OK then."

"I'll have the same." I said this as if I'd ordered it a hundred times when I'd never eaten an egg in my life that wasn't scrambled. But it seemed as if everything ought to change somehow, especially since I was somebody else already and had not slept in my bed the night before. I hadn't counted on being the only one with money, but then nothing so far was happening the way I thought it would.

For the first time I thought of my father walking into my empty room, picking up the note. I watched him as he touched my hair on the paper and felt the stricture in his chest as he saw the open window and realized how like him I'd become.

We spent the day sitting by the water, mostly waiting for the night.

"Are your folks looking for you?" Luke asked.

"My father."

"Not your mother?"

"No."

"Is she dead, or just gone?"

A tug, escorted by a flock of seagulls, pushed an empty barge toward the open bay. The engine throbbed, its steady strokes reverberating off the water's flat surface. I watched it go until it was just a speck on the water, a black tail of blurred smoke trailing behind.

"Just . . . gone," I said.

"But would she look for you if she *knew* you were gone?" He seemed intent on finding out, as if he'd never met anyone who'd been missed enough to be searched for.

Would she? "Sure," I told him. To myself, I honestly

couldn't say. A thought threw itself over me like a wide net: the one person in the world who had always known where I was, even when I was out of sight, was now moving steadily out of range of my voice. If she had one thought left, it was for my father, I was certain, that his call was the one loud enough to be heard, that could crash its way into the hospital, into heaven or hell if it had to make its way inside her still-listening ear.

Night came on slowly, and the dark blue seeped down into the yellow horizon the way ink blends into water. Lights of the ship flashed on; a constellation gradually revealed itself. We watched the crew come down the ramp for dinner, laughing and jostling each other through the door into the diner.

We stood close to the ship without a clue as to how to get on it or where to go once we did. The beam of a flashlight cut through the dark above the deck. We couldn't see the hand that held it. The beam swept in a long arc toward us, as if it knew we were there, and sliced through us as easily as the blade of a magician's saw. We stood, frozen, transfixed as deer in the sudden light. Someone at the other end of it hollered, and we ran for the tall grass behind us.

The marsh sucked at our shoes, and cattails slapped against us as we ran. Gradually, the ground got firmer, the grass tapered down, and we came up an embankment to a railroad track. The sharp smell of creosote hung in the air. Luke put his ear down on the rail, which shone like a blade in the light from the rising moon, and listened for the vibration of an engine down the line. I knelt there too, my ear

against the cold steel, and far off, I could feel, more than
hear it — long before the light flared down the tracks — the
train coming. I put a penny down, out of habit; then we
backed away over the edge of the bank and lay next to each
other. The rails quivered with the weight of at least a hundred wheels.

"You have to jump high, grab a rung with at least one
hand to get on," Luke shouted above the blast of the whistle. "Leave the suitcase here."

I looked at it lying in the grass, the decals faintly glossed
with light. I dug my fingers into the ground, poised like a
runner, my body a spring, glad to have simple instructions
to follow. But the train was too far from any junction or
crossing that could have slowed it down, and we watched it
pass — wheels and streaks of space between wheels — giving out a sound we couldn't even scream over. Then it was
gone, trailing a red light behind. We watched it disappear
into a tunnel or around a bend and heard the far-off sound
of a crossing bell ringing its tinny warning down the tracks.
Luke just stood there looking defeated, as if the whole
world was beyond him. "I thought it would slow down," he
said. "I really did."

"It's OK," I said. "There's bound to be another one."

I pictured the black-and-white-striped arms going down
at the nearest crossing, the red flashing eye in the black,
staring socket, and remembered a time in the car with my
father and mother. The bell was clanging, the train coming,
the arms lowering, and instead of stopping, my father tried
to get through the crossing before it closed. I heard the
thud of the arm on the roof of the car, heard the splintered

crack as we broke through, heard my mother's voice rising in anger, "Now why, why on earth did you do that?" My father didn't answer and the train thundered behind us, the first danger we had brushed up against. Unlike my mother, I was not afraid but felt a strange, unholy thrill at his having taken such a risk and come away unharmed.

When I woke it was not really light yet. I looked up and the sky was a watery blue; a star — Venus probably — burned as bright as the point of paper under a magnifying glass just before it turns to fire.

Luke and I were wrapped around each other, though I didn't remember how we got that way, that motion in the dark toward the warmth of another. The next train never did come, and we fell asleep waiting for it. The grass, a foot high around the place we'd flattened with our bodies, was bent over with the weight of dew. We stood up, shivering, and looked behind us to the diner down the hill, its red and white sign just coming on, flickering, uncertain at first, then holding steady. Behind it, we could see the empty place on the water where the ship had been.

Luke turned away from the water. "New York, that's the place. This is a low-class port, just freighters. In New York they've got ocean liners — we'll have a better chance."

I remembered my father telling me about sailing on the maiden voyage of the Queen Mary from New York to South-ampton, much later than his first voyage. He had money then, and a job waiting for him at the other end.

We headed on foot in the general direction of New York, and it wasn't long before we found a highway. We

didn't stand there any longer than fifteen minutes with our
thumbs out before a truck stopped and we climbed up on
the wheel. Luke pulled me into the cab after him. The
driver didn't look that much older than Luke — red hair in a
crew cut, aviator sunglasses, a tattoo of a mermaid that
swam on his bicep as he shifted the gears.

"I'm headed for Queens," he shouted above the straining engine.

"Is that near New York City?" I asked.

"Close enough."

Queens, *Queen Mary* — it all seemed related.

"Eighteen of these," he said proudly, as he shifted.
"That's why it's such a drag to stop once you get rolling.
You're lucky I did, but hey, I could use the company. I just
did three days from L.A. alone, just me and my white crosses." He paused to take a breath. "Goddamn," he said, as if
after three thousand miles he still couldn't comprehend
how he'd gotten there.

We came into Brooklyn by the Verrazano Bridge, and
soon Brooklyn was gone and we were in Queens, though
we crossed no border that I could see. It was late afternoon
when he let us off near the East River. He saluted us and
grinned, then hauled through at least four of the eighteen
gears before he turned a corner and drove out of sight.

We stood on the cobblestone street. A soupy kind of
breeze floated in off the river, scented with garbage and
sewage and brine. We walked in that direction. By this time
Luke was holding my hand. He'd squeezed it once in the
truck when we got our first glimpse of the Empire State
Building from the Jersey side, and now he took my hand on

faith that I would not pull away, that there was enough between us to justify the touch. And I liked the feel of his hand. It was rough and warm and surprisingly strong.

There were people out on stoops because it was so hot, kids leaping like marionettes in the plumes of water gushing from open hydrants.

We bought some hot dogs from a vendor with a shiny silver cart that sprouted a red and yellow umbrella. He painted them with catsup and mustard.

"The works?" he asked and we watched the dogs disappear under a hill of onions and relish. When he handed me my change I asked him, "Is the *Queen Mary* around here?"

He laughed. "Where you been, Timbuktu? She sailed for the scrap heap a long time ago. Why, you got a ticket?"

He laughed so hard he went into a sneezing fit. I counted nine as we walked away.

Suddenly I felt so tired I didn't think I could move another step. Queens stretched out in too many directions, and I wanted to be out to sea, rocked by waves on the long voyage. I wanted, after the crossing, to smell land, the sweet smoke and earth of Ireland where my father said our people came from, and walk ashore to a place where my name would be as common as the trees.

As we got closer to the river, its scent grew stronger, and we came out of the canyons of red brick warehouses into the glaring light on the East River, a body of water as silver and thick as mercury, heavy and waveless, with ships ploughing through it toward the white glare of the open harbor.

The ships in port were not liners strung with small

colored flags. There were no crowds of people leaning from
the deck flinging handfuls of pink confetti onto the heads of
the people who waved below. The ship we wanted was sideways, chained to the iron teeth of the dock, the word *Gal-*
way in faded letters across its stern. Cranes were swinging
crates as big as houses. We stood there in the shade of it,
watching the loading. I tried to imagine a place inside that
hollow, ringing steel that could hide us.

I heard a sound I had heard only once before in my life,
at the Bronx zoo: a wild, trumpeting call. It was an elephant, led backward from a truck down a wooden ramp. It
stood on the asphalt, shivering with terror, while two men
looped a cloth cinch as big as a sheet beneath its belly. A
large hook was threaded through the grommets at the top,
and the crane's engine roared with the sound a Ferris wheel
makes when it starts up. The cable grew taut. The elephant
rolled its eyes back. As the cable pulled up, the elephant
seemed to stretch its legs down, trying to keep them planted firmly on the ground. With a jerk, the crane pulled hard
and the elephant's feet left the earth, its knees buckling
slightly, while the legs, as sturdy as trees on the ground,
swung helplessly, testing the terrifying emptiness around
them. Its trunk lifted, and the animal let out a sound that
should have stopped the world. But the crane swung its
steel arm over the deck and the elephant dangled over the
hold, then disappeared deep inside the ship, where it continued to call, the sound echoing mournfully off the steel
hull until it sounded as if the ship itself were crying out in
terror. I thought about what would happen at the other
end, and all I could see was the elephant, swinging, a weary

shape in the gray, indefinite air of Ireland, coming down onto a terrain that once again would not be home.

I looked at Luke's stricken face, saw that he was crying. He wiped his eyes with the sleeve of his denim jacket, which left a faint gray smear across his cheek. I looked at him in wonder, for inside myself, there was a ricocheting howl that could not find its way to an open mouth to let it out. Luke, at least, had tears, even though he didn't make a sound.

There was no way I could turn back. I was convinced that if I just got on the ship it would be all right, but for the first time I couldn't picture what might happen when I got to Ireland. My father had never made it to Dublin, though that's where he wanted to go — his story trailed off somewhere in Belfast. Did he even get off the ship when it docked?

It was dark and still when we made our move. We had loaded the suitcase with as many provisions as it would hold: candy bars, cans of root beer, oranges. We thought it would be enough to tide us over, though neither of us could guess how long the voyage might be. It would have to be enough. We were out of money.

Luke's knowledge ended at the foot of the gangway, and neither of us knew what to expect from there on in. We crouched low and started to crawl along the wooden ramp. I grabbed on to a corner of his jacket and held the suitcase tight against my chest. We were almost to the deck when a voice behind us said, "Well, now." Light crawled over our bodies from a flashlight. "Going somewhere?" The voice was husky, slow. The man had a lot of time. I could hear him strike a match, draw on a cigarette, let the smoke out in a satisfied way.

"Tell you what." He exhaled again. I could smell it now, and it stung my nose. "I won't call the cops." I halfway turned around but couldn't see his face, just the glaring disk of light and his vague shape behind it. "I can help you get on . . . You look like you could use a meal, a bath, maybe a little sleep? I got a house in Jersey. Bring you back first thing."

He turned off the light, and then I could see him more clearly. Gray hair and glasses. A man about my father's age.

"Come on — my shift is up. You kids look beat. Car's right across the street." He took the suitcase from me. "How old are you?"

"Eighteen," I lied.

"You?" he said, nodding at Luke.

"Same."

He seemed pleased with our answers.

We walked across the empty loading dock. The crane was silent. The elephant was silent. We walked toward the man's car, a red and white Oldsmobile, a sleek thing crouched in the dark. The man unlocked it, held the door open. I looked at Luke for some signal to break and run, some corroboration of the vague uneasiness I was feeling, trying to guess whether the man's words hid something he wasn't saying. But Luke slid across the seat, so I slid in next to him. I was still traveling hopefully, but it was getting harder all the time.

"I went to Atlantic City once — always wanted to go back," Luke said to him.

"I live in Newark. No boardwalk there. No ocean neither. Just a shitty little river." He jabbed the key into the lock. The automatic transmission clicked into a single, simple gear called Drive and we headed west across the Hudson.

There was a yard with trees, borders of white flowers. The door opened easily to his key. He put my suitcase down in the hallway. On a narrow table where he set down his keys, there was a picture of a girl with dark wings of hair around a heart-shaped face, younger than me. There was a dog, a gray poodle, happy to be touched and fed.

He turned the radio on. He told us to sit at the table while he got us something to eat. Cold chicken, potato salad from a plastic bowl with daisies on it. Lemonade in jelly-jar glasses. We waited for him to sit down before we ate. And then we tried to eat as if we had all the time in the world.

He took me upstairs after dinner. "Here's a clean towel," he said. "You can take your bath now."

I closed the door behind me. I turned on the water and the tub filled fast. I got in, submerged myself up to my chin and leaned back, my head resting on the hard, curved arm of the porcelain tub. I closed my eyes.

The door opened, then closed again.

"Stand up," he said. "I want to see what you look like."

At first I didn't move, then I rose slowly out of the water, pulled by a command that I hadn't figured out how to refuse, afraid, too, of what would happen if I didn't do as he told me.

I stood there dripping. I looked at the wall behind him, purple violets and green leaves on pale pink paper. It was peeling away from the wall around the light switch like sunburned skin. Don't look at me, I thought. Then I remembered something I'd read about Hindus, how bathing is sacred and private for them even when they're publicly naked in a river, and so they're invisible while they're in the water. I felt that as long as I didn't look at him I couldn't really be seen.

"Beauty mark," he said, and smiled.

But I had no beauty mark. The door opened, then clicked shut. I sank slowly down into the warm water again. And then I noticed something — a dark spot on my stomach. I touched it with the tip of my finger. It was stuck tight, didn't move. A tick. I shuddered but left it there. I smiled to think how I fooled him — I thought it could protect me like a charm, that he wouldn't touch me if he saw it up close, if he found out that what he thought was a mark of beauty was in fact a thing that bit and crawled.

Luke was sitting on the couch with a girl our age when I came back downstairs. They were both laughing and drinking red wine out of a bottle, passing it back and forth. The man sat in a chair, his face flushed red with the wine, watching them intently.

"Judy here used to be my baby-sitter when my daughter was little."

Judy barely nodded in my direction. She kicked off her shoes and propped her feet on the coffee table, nearly knocking over a green metal ashtray full of crushed white filters and gray ash.

"Lou," she said to him. "Lou, give the lady a drink. You can't come to the party if you don't have a drink." She twisted her long black hair around her index finger repeatedly, as if she were teaching it to curl and it was slow in learning.

The man poured me a glass of sweet wine. I tried to catch Luke's eye, but Luke raised the bottle in the air and grinned. "Down the hatch, Luce."

I just stared at him, and then remembered Luz was the name I'd picked for myself. Suddenly I wanted to tell him my real name, and I almost did, but it seemed the only thing I could keep to myself anymore.

"You have to drink it all," the man said to me as if he were telling a child to clean her plate or she couldn't get up from the table.

I drank the glass dry. I kept glancing at Luke, looking for signals, but he was giving me none. He'd pulled inside himself; he couldn't really see me anymore.

I sat down on the floor, leaned against the coffee table, and closed my eyes. I felt as if I were swimming, the way I did the summer my mother taught me the breaststroke. She taught me to swim all the way out to the raft on the lake where we used to live. She would dive cleanly into the water from the dock, and I would smack the water with my belly as I followed. "Truly graceful, Matty," she said as she backstroked away from me. She stood on the raft, dripping, hands on her narrow hips as I struggled with the last fifty yards. She was shouting some instructions to me, but I couldn't hear above my own splashing. She reached her hand toward me as I came alongside, gasping for air, and pulled me up to the light and sun-warmed planks. We lay there, face up for a time, listening to the soft slap of water against the oil-drum pontoons.

Her breathing grew deeper, rhythmic, and soon she was asleep. She "went under" as she would call it, and I pictured her in the green water below, diving toward a deeper green, where the water lilies attached their long swaying cords to the silted bottom. I felt protective of her, as if my vigilance while she swam alone through that other world could be a homing signal she would return to, helping her ascend slowly from the sickness toward the bright surface and break through into the warm, sweet air.

When I opened my eyes, Judy and the man were gone. Luke was leaning over me.

"Look — I'm going to get him to go for me instead of you," he said.

"What are you *saying?*"

"I've done this. I can do it again."

All evening I'd been looking to him for clues, and now he'd already decided on the final outcome, to exchange the currency of his body for mine. He wasn't steady on his feet, and his breath was heavy with the sweet-sour stench of wine. He could barely stand up — he wasn't about to make a run for it. Whatever map I'd started this trip with had been torn in half. I had no idea where to go. I felt so stunned, I lost my fear and could no longer read any of the signals around me.

The man came out of the kitchen with another bottle; this time it was scotch. He grabbed Luke by the back of the collar. "Get upstairs," he said roughly to Luke. Then his voice became teasing, "Judy's waiting for you."

Luke backed away from me, his eyes almost dreamy, his body tilting as if trying to right itself against a crosswind. He made his way up the stairs, holding the railing the whole way. The man lurched toward me, his fatherly demeanor completely gone. He seemed angry and grabbed my hair at the back of my neck like a mane, yanked it so that I had to stand up.

He hauled me up the stairs by my hair, what little there was left. I thought about how glad I was that I'd cut it before I left. I concentrated on being too heavy to move, on sending down roots into the floor. But still I moved. At the top of the stairs he pushed a door open and thrust me into the room.

"Take a good look. See how much your boyfriend loves you now."

At first all I could see was an aquarium, the darting, shadowy shapes of angelfish threading through bubbles that rose from a tiny figure of a man in a diving bell. Behind the aquarium something moved, and as my eyes grew accustomed to the dark I saw Luke and Judy, their skin green in the watery light, their bodies heaving with a rhythm that was loveless, urgent, mean. I leaned against the wall, my eyes closed against them all. Everything was changing, too fast for me to understand. I didn't know who was on whose side any longer.

He twisted my arm behind my back until I thought it

would surely break. "That's what I'm going to do to you," he said, just inches from my ear.

He shoved me into the hallway and into a dark room. I fell back against a bed. I found my voice and yelled, but it was a thin shield that couldn't stop anything from getting through. Even the sound of his zipper tore through the air. When he fell on me, I was sure every bone inside me would break.

A gray light seeped into the room. I woke up alone. There was a single drop of blood on the white sheet that I couldn't believe came from me. I yanked the covers over it, ashamed, as I had been the day four years ago when I'd worn my coat all day in a hot classroom to hide the sudden evidence of my first menstrual flow, indelibly red on the back of my white wool skirt.

I got up slowly, crawled on the floor to find my clothes. I listened, my ear to the door. The house was utterly still. Luke was somewhere down the hall, probably asleep with Judy, and it made me sick to think of it. The man had slept in some other room, or on the couch downstairs. I looked around me. White ruffled curtains, a pile of stuffed animals on a window seat. On the dresser, a blue jewelry box. I opened it and a ballerina spun silently on a mirror, whatever music that had once moved her broken inside the music box. I closed the lid. I opened it again. Again the noiseless dance. A slender silver bracelet with a turquoise heart set in its center lay in a velvet compartment all by itself. I tried it on. It fit. I didn't put it back.

The window was impossible to open — storm windows

were wedged into the sill from the outside. I shielded my eyes and kicked. It broke with a terrific crash. I kept kicking it till I made a space wide enough to crawl through. It was like leaving through a mouth with jagged teeth. It took everything I had left — it still does — to stop the shouting in my head: "Why didn't you do this last night? Why didn't you get away?"

I broke into a wild run when I hit the ground, down the tree-lined street, until I came to a busy intersection. I stuck out my thumb. I only had one thought left, and Luke was no longer in it. If I ran to the police they would call my father — I couldn't let that happen. I was not done yet. I had to get back to Sparrow's Point, to start over, to get it right this time.

A girl in a sports car picked me up, and the Beatles were turned up loud on the radio singing "Love Me Do." Her hair was wound around pink curlers, a yellow scarf tied over it all.

"Cuttin' school?"

I nodded.

She smiled.

"I used to do that so much they finally told me to stay home for good. But I showed them — I got a job as a teller at the bank and saved up 'til I got this car."

I was so relieved I could have cried — there she was talking to me as if I was just a normal person. I drank in all the bright details of her as if I had a sudden, unslakable thirst and she had just handed me a dipper full of water.

"I'm going to Philly," she said, "to see my boyfriend."

"I have to get to Baltimore." I was afraid she would ask me why, but she just grinned at me.

"Sorry I can't get you all the way there, but it's a start anyway." She lit a cigarette with the dashboard lighter. "Long way to go to cut school."

She handed me a sack of sugared donuts and passed me a bottle of Coke she had wedged between the bucket seats.

At the tollgate to the turnpike she took the ticket and I leaned my head back in the seat and fell asleep as she sang along with the Rolling Stones on the radio.

She woke me at a rest stop. "I get off just up ahead — you can find a ride here, no problem. Have a great time!"

She roared off, then waved her hand out the window as she looked into her rearview mirror.

I hadn't stood there two minutes when a highway patrol car pulled up next to me.

"Which car here belongs to you?" he asked.

I stared at him, trying to find the right expression — bored, annoyed, incensed?

"Thought so. You'll have to come with me." He opened the back door.

He put me in a holding cell at the precinct station. There was an iron bed without a mattress or a blanket. Someone brought me a cup of coffee and a hamburger. Someone said, "Matty, we've called your father." Somehow, they knew exactly who I was. The thing is, when the police-woman escorted me to the bathroom, and I looked into the mirror above the rusted, dripping sink, I really didn't recognize myself anymore.

"Well, well — thirteen-state alarm, TV and all. Think you're pretty smart, don't you? We'll check you, you know," she said with a confident sneer. "We'll have a doctor find out if you did anything — you know what I mean."

Suddenly I was more terrified than at any point on the whole trip. I didn't want anyone to know, didn't want that part to ruin my story. I was afraid my own body would finally betray me, would break the silence that was all I had to keep.

The radio was on all night long. I couldn't imagine what was taking my father so long unless he thought he was teaching me a lesson by making me spend the night in jail. The cops came in with prostitutes at three in the morning. They all had long legs and lots of teased hair — blond or jet black, never brown. The lights stayed on, neon buzzing in the tubes like flies trapped in a jar. There was no such thing as privacy. If you asked for anything, the cops said, "What do you think this is, the Hilton Hotel?" It was their standard joke. They wanted to remind you every minute that you were in their hands, that there was no choice other than to do what they told you.

I pictured my father getting in the car, revving the engine too much to warm it, backing out of the driveway and nearly hitting the gatepost. He knocked it down once. For months there was a pile of white bricks at the edge of the driveway. Grass grew up between them, snow covered the whole mess, and the grass returned once more before he got around to hiring someone to build it back the way it was.

I thought about my father driving the interstate, which he'd always avoided, preferring the back roads and blue highways, peering at the unfamiliar green signs, looking at a scribbled note on the seat beside him where I was not sitting to remind him, as I always did, of the right turn to make, when it looked safe to pass. He was traveling on my road now — six lanes of traffic along the eastern seaboard. Trucks were bearing down on him, riding his tail and pulling sharply around and ahead of him. I felt his fear, his awkwardness in coming such a distance to find me.

In the early morning a policeman steered me by the elbow to a room with a single chair in it. "Wait here" was all he said.

I slouched in the chair and looked at my hands, noticed how dirty my fingernails were, how my clothes looked as if I'd lived in them for years. I heard voices coming through the open door from the next room. One voice was my father's, but I couldn't hear what he was saying.

The sergeant led me into another room. I saw my father across that room, a man smaller than I remembered, older too. Neither of us moved toward the other.

I looked away from him, at the light coming through the window, how it made a yellow, fractured rectangle on the floor as it squeezed through the half-open blinds. I waited, frozen to a spot on the floor. Then I looked at him. We faced each other, my father and I across that room, as if a mire of quicksand lay in between.

My father rose unsteadily from the chair. He stood there, hands at his sides, fingers opening and closing, opening and closing.

"Oh, Matty," he said, not much above a whisper, more to himself than to me.

We didn't say anything at all as we walked to the car. I kept waiting for him to talk, but for once he seemed at a complete loss for words. He opened the door, and I slid into the passenger seat. My father pumped the accelerator, and the engine turned over, sluggish, the battery nearly drained because he'd left the lights on. But it started on the second try, and he steered slowly, cautiously, out of the parking lot into the crowded street. It was dusk, but light enough still to see his face — a gray mask that revealed nothing of what he was thinking or feeling. I watched the row houses, the lights of their kitchens, and the outlines of women moving through them. There were vacant lots with kids playing stickball, lifting their heads when someone called them home to dinner.

The highway was dark in the long stretches between exits. I cleared my throat, but let another exit go by before I opened my mouth. "How's Mom?" I asked.

"Better," he said. "Better. But I didn't tell her anything about this — and don't you, either. This isn't what she needs to hear right now."

I had only that one chance — a specific number of miles between where we were and the driveway. If I didn't tell it then, I never would. So I began. I told him about Sparrow's Point, the ship, except I told about the elephant then instead of the place it really was. I thought that since it was my story I could tell it the way I wanted. I tried to tell it as if it had been the adventure I had in mind — that's what people needed to hear. He listened, both hands on the wheel for once because he wasn't doing the talking. He was paying attention now. Words were spilling from me and I couldn't stop. I told about the diner, about eating fried eggs, about the truck and the train. I left Luke out of it because I didn't want him there, and because, simply by omission, I could erase him, and when I got to the part about Queens and New Jersey and all that happened there, the words trickled down to nothing. And then I just stopped talking altogether.

It grew completely dark. Our hands and knees were lit by the green glow of the dashboard dials, our expressions diffused in underwater light.

He paid the toll, dropped his ticket stub on the floor, and drove over the long span of the Delaware Bridge. There was a ship below, heading out of the mouth of the river into the black Atlantic, away from the lights of the bridge, the city below. Any other time the sight of a ship would bring on the story of the *Nora*. This time he let it go as if he knew what words could set in motion, that he would not risk telling me anything like it again. Now we both had stories we couldn't tell.

We crossed the state of Maryland without a single word. And still a hundred miles from home, I felt my father begin to veer away from me as if in that narrow space and silence we might somehow collide.

I leaned my face against the window. There was a moon. I could see the familiar landmarks of the Blue Ridge Mountains slowly rise to meet us in the distance, the Potomac River running toward the Shenandoah, whose name my mother always loved to say, to Harper's Ferry, where they would soon converge. The words were gone so soon, the story good for just a single telling. Then I began to feel the heat of my own breath, see the evidence of it on the window, and I made it bloom again and again on the mirrored glass.

There is no one listening now but me. I haven't skipped a single thing. Except that I don't feel a single thing. I sit here, emptied out, surprised that after all that compression it doesn't tear me open on its way out.

A cactus wren squawks from the prickly pear cactus bush behind me. It zings straight into the sliding glass door, and with a small cracking noise that doesn't affect the glass at all, the bird drops to the flagstone. It doesn't move. I walk over and pick it up. It's warm, motionless, its eyes still open.

A small death is what finally breaks me. I sit here, weeping, holding the bird in my hands for the longest time. Now that I've started, it seems I will be doing this forever.

Then the bird stirs in my hands. I open them and the thing flies. I feel tricked and stop crying immediately. I wipe my face on my sleeve and watch it go. I fully expect it to falter, to fall. But it flies. It flies, most assuredly, away.

Della's voice comes from far away, strained and desperate through the phone.

"Della, I can't hear you."

She says to someone, "You'll have to hold it closer."

She can't even hold a telephone anymore, which also means she can't hold a trowel or a spoon, or a glass bead. She has lost her most precious possessions — her own two hands.

"Can you hear me better now?"

My voice feels thick, unused, weak. "Are you all right?"

"I need to go to the store. Margaret's out of town and won't be back till tomorrow."

"When?"

"Now. This minute." Her voice fades, moves farther away. "You can hang up now." At first I think she's talking to me, but she says it to the person holding the phone for her. I try to imagine what that person is doing — reading a magazine, watching TV? — trying not to listen while Della carries on a conversation just inches away.

It's the first time Della has asked me for anything. She's so pushy about it that it rankles me. Everything's always on her terms, in her own time. Still, it doesn't seem right to refuse her.

When I get to the house, I can see how Margaret's presence has already changed it. Her son's bike, flung on its side, blocks the path Della and I had made. Bursts of canned laughter from a TV spill out the door.

A woman in a nurse's uniform comes to let me in. She whispers to me as I step inside, "You don't have to do this — it's certainly not necessary." The nurse points at Della. "She's headstrong. Shouldn't always get her way."

Della stands in the middle of the room, fenced in by the small corral of a walker. She inches toward me, the wheels squeaking like a toy.

"Get me out of here," Della mutters under her breath, scowling with every excruciating step.

I've never helped a handicapped person before, and I'm quickly confronted with the world of half-inch obstacles — the mountains of doorsills, the immovable walls of car doors. I have to extricate the walker, which snags on the door handle after she heaves herself none-too-gracefully into the front seat.

I buckle Della in.

"Just drive — I'll tell you where to go." She sits there, tense as a drawn bow. The truck rocks through the pot-holes, the walker crashes around in the back. Her body relaxes only slightly as we turn onto the main road, and she thrusts her elbow out the open window when I finally get to fourth gear.

"I'm not going to the store." She says this matter-of-fact-ly, looking straight ahead through the windshield. Strands of hair teased out of their pins and combs by the wind are floating wild around her.

"Take me to the airport and help me get a ticket to New York."

"What do you mean New York — you don't have any-thing with you. It might help if you *asked* instead of told me what to do." I know that logic and common courtesy are ludicrous in this situation, but it's the only way I can think of to respond.

"Well, I couldn't just pack myself a bag, now could I? Do you really think that woman in my house would let me go?" She twists around in the seat, pulling the seat belt away from her chest. "I can't stand these things." She's practically shouting now. "My house — my lovely house, got turned into a madhouse overnight. And that boy, that Daryl, has junked up the place with TV noise. I can't think straight anymore. The only peace left is in the middle of the night — I stay awake just so I can have it."

"Can't you ask your daughter to go back to her own place? Goddamn it, Della, *I'll* tell her to leave."

"She got evicted; she's got no husband, no money. I can't just put her out." She throws one of those gnarled, misshapen hands in the air and the gesture looks more like an ancient curse than the capitulation that should match her voice. "The place'll be hers soon enough anyway; she might as well start moving her things in now. I'm through here."

She slumps down in the seat as if the very idea of it defeats her. "What bothers me more than anything is leaving without finishing it — it looks like something bombed out in the war, that arch going just halfway. It's unseemly. It was going to be the best part."

"I know all about that — half-telling, not finishing."

She studies me, waits for me to put in my two cents' worth, but I've said what I needed to say. It's her turn, anyway, to be put on the spot, so I fire another question at her. "Do you know anybody in New York, Della?"

"Do I know anybody in New York? Have I taken complete leave of my senses? I have a friend there — she's got lupus and has a live-in nurse she actually likes. We can put our money together. We can, thank you very much, live as we damn well please."

"But does she *know* you're coming?" Now I'm shouting. I nearly sideswipe a Pepsi truck.

"I've got a standing invitation," she says, with a regal, haughty, toss of her head. Then she's angry again. "I couldn't call her up, now could I, with a nurse holding the phone to my head."

"What about the plane ticket? Jesus, Della . . ."

"Plastic — they sent it to me in the mail — can you believe it — they'll give credit to anyone these days, even a nasty old woman like me.

"But I'm not crazy," she says, defiantly turning to me as if her very expression could convince me. "Everyone else gets to pick up and go. Look at you! Now it's my turn. *Mine!*"

"It's not like you think, Della. Just you wait. You get out there, things go wrong."

"Things go wrong anyway, whether you're moving or not." She's impatient, as if I've missed the point.

I take my eyes off the road for just a second so I can look at her. It's as if she's reached right in to yank out the last loose thread that's keeping everything I've remembered these past weeks from making sense.

Someone in a van blasts his horn when I cut him off. I blast him back.

"Will you slow down and pay attention — you're going to kill me before we get there. I never said to hurry. And stop looking so shocked and sad — you should see yourself."

I ease off on the gas, but inside, I'm floored, racing,

revved. There's something loose inside me — an almost uncontrollable urge to stop. Once and for all, but, as always, an equal desire to break and run.

"Della, am I supposed to talk you out of this?" But I know there aren't words to stop people — Ben had never found the right ones, or maybe he had, and I ignored them anyway.

"Of course not," she says, then laughs. "You've got more spunk than I thought, more than my daughter. Why didn't I get one like you?"

"You wouldn't have kept me around either," I say.

"Probably not," she says. "But then again, maybe so."

She manages to get her seat belt off before the truck comes to a complete stop at the curb. I imagine she's the kind of passenger flight attendants will have to reprimand for disobeying the seat belt sign. I lift the walker out and set it up, then lean down to help her out.

"Use my shoulder."

"I was *going* to." She's getting more surly by the minute.

She hoists herself up and falls against me. We rock unsteadily. "Don't let go of me — I don't want to fall. Not here, not today." She's almost pleading now.

A police officer walks quickly toward us. For a moment I'm certain there's an APB out on us, maybe even a thirteen-state alarm, that the nurse has turned us in.

"Do you need wheelchair assistance?" he asks. "I can call a skycap."

Della winces. She must be calculating the huge distance

from herself to the gate. "That would be most helpful," she says, as if she were long accustomed to such arrangements.

A wheelchair glides toward us, and I take it from the skycap, tell him I want to push her myself. He says it's highly irregular, that he can get in trouble. Della tells him *we* are highly irregular, and that if there's any trouble with his boss, he should come to her.

After I sign Della's name on the credit card receipt, we make our way through security and park ourselves at the gate in front of one of the huge windows flanking the door. In less than an hour she will disappear. I stand behind her, gripping the handles. A plane sits on the runway, waiting to be released.

"Well," I say, "there's no going back now."

For once, she doesn't have a snappy comeback. She seems a little beaten down by all this. She nods her head. "Who would want to?" she says quietly.

She turns halfway around. Her profile takes me by surprise — the utter beauty of it, the elegance of her uplifted chin, the ribbony folds of the skin on her neck, the wide-open blue of her eyes, radiant with determination, the way she seems to offer her face to me — not to kiss, but to take in her countenance so that it will be remembered. She turns back to the window. I let go of the wheelchair handles and stretch my fingers from their cramped grip. My hands move forward until they rest lightly on her shoulders — hard and smooth as polished marble, but warm beneath her blue cotton shirt. I want more than anything to undo her hair, for that silver hair to come down gladly into my hands. I tremble as I reach for one of the pins. Then I stop. For once in my life, I let the impulse ride. Instead, I bring my hands back to her shoulders, knead the muscles gently. She starts, surprised. "Let me." I bend close to say it. And she doesn't try to stop me; she stares straight ahead. Her head drops forward slightly, inviting me to stay.

She straightens up after a while, and I take it as a signal to stop. My hands feel warm. Stretched. Strong.

As if he has stood by waiting, the skycap appears out of nowhere when the preliminary boarding is announced and takes her from me.

"Della!" I call after her. The skycap pauses as he wheels her down the jetway. I'm sure she heard me, and for a minute I think she'll ask him to turn her around so she can say something, but that's not what she does. She raises her hand high enough so I'll be sure to notice it. I raise my own when she's out of sight.

I sit on my patio with my camera in my lap in the late afternoon. The first real monsoon storm of the summer builds to the southeast. I watch the cumulus clouds gather out of thin air. Lightning pulses inside them, but they're too far away; I can't hear their thunder.

I look down at my feet, propped up on the low table in front of me. So, there's that foot again — the perfect photographic subject. Like Della, I'm down to making do. I bring the camera to my eye. Through the lens, I travel the enormous distance from my toes to the arch of my foot and stop. My focus is so tight that what comes through the viewfinder doesn't look at all like a foot — the arch smooth as sandstone, high enough for a river to pass beneath; the ankle a low hill traversed by indigo veins. Two hairs I missed shaving. The scorpion bite now a slight, red scar, healed.

I set the camera on the tripod and guess at focus. I have no idea what the film will record. Anyone walking down the road would see an odd ritual, a naked woman playing musical chairs by herself, walking behind the camera, pressing the shutter, then running like mad in front of the lens to pose and freeze. But no one comes down the road. Della's at thirty-nine thousand feet now, home free.

I work late into the night and make at least thirty eight-by-ten prints, then spread them out on the living room floor. I sort through the pile like Psyche, putting the things that belong together together. A puzzle. It's haphazard, doesn't really fit together. A makeshift kind of thing, like Della's weird collages. A map of my own body, reassembled from the torn pieces that fell from Ben's window.

My vision comes back to me, of course, when I'm no longer looking. I've never seen my back before — straight on without twisting — but there it is, bent slightly forward so the vertebrae make a narrow stairway upward toward my hair. My hair is longer than I realized — my mother's hair, touching my shoulders, coming down to me. There are my father's strong-fingered hands. Jack's mouth — the resemblance is striking — slightly open, not quite smiling, not quite sad. And, like no one else's, Matty Grover's eyes.

Della's nurse drives down the hill. No one else goes up. I drive to the house one more time.

Just me now, mixing the mud and straw in Della's bucket. Yellow light clings to the ridgeline of the Tucson Mountains for a long time — plenty of light to work by.

Della's arch is a little more than halfway completed,
framed by a lintel of adobe bricks. It's lopsided, but strong.
I pull some stones from the pile she left, sorting through
them until I find ones that fit together. Despite their rela-
tively small size, they're heavier than I thought.

The mud comes easily to the right consistency as I mix
the water slowly — I learned that from watching her. I drag
a bench over to where I can put everything I need on top of
it. I climb up. On the bottom of the lintel, I spread some
mud, then place the stone. It stays for a grand total of ten
seconds, then crashes to the walkway below. I feel inept, ill
prepared. I don't understand the principles involved in arch-
es, which laws of physics prevail. I decide to emulate Della
— improvise. In back of the house there's more junk than I
thought possible for a person to possess. But I guess that's
the bane and bonus of staying put — you save everything
because maybe there's an eventual use for all of it. There's a
pile of weathered two-by-fours, and I pick out several, of
varying lengths.

Picking out one that seems the right length, I prop it
beneath the stone I just put back in place in the still-soft
mud.

It's nearly dark when I finish. I step down from the
bench, wipe my hands on my shirttails. Standing at arm's
length, I take hold of the first support. I close my eyes and
pull. I wait a long time. The stone holds. It holds. One last
trowel of mud at the apex of the arch. On tiptoe, I press my

palms there to sign it. Both of our names, one for each hand, which seems only fair.

When the coyotes start up, they could be laughing, or crying, or announcing a kill, or just calling to their own kind.

I hear it, Della, as wild and raucous praise.

Alison Moore lives in the desert outside Tucson, and she teaches fiction writing in the University of Arizona's Creative Writing Program. She is publications director for ArtsReach, a nonprofit organization dedicated to teaching creative writing to Native American children. She was a recipient of a 1993 NEA creative writing fellowship. Her work has appeared in *Ms.* magazine, *Story Magazine,* and an anthology entitled *Southwest Stories.*